Eclipse of Easter Island

Eclipse of Easter Island

An Ethan Sparks Adventure

Nick Barry

ECLIPSE OF EASTER ISLAND
AN ETHAN SPARKS ADVENTURE

Copyright © 2015 Nick Barry.

All rights reserved. No part of this book may be used or reproduced by any means, graphic, electronic, or mechanical, including photocopying, recording, taping or by any information storage retrieval system without the written permission of the publisher except in the case of brief quotations embodied in critical articles and reviews.

This is a work of fiction. All of the characters, names, incidents, organizations, and dialogue in this novel are either the products of the author's imagination or are used fictitiously.

iUniverse books may be ordered through booksellers or by contacting:

iUniverse
1663 Liberty Drive
Bloomington, IN 47403
www.iuniverse.com
1-800-Authors (1-800-288-4677)

Because of the dynamic nature of the Internet, any web addresses or links contained in this book may have changed since publication and may no longer be valid. The views expressed in this work are solely those of the author and do not necessarily reflect the views of the publisher, and the publisher hereby disclaims any responsibility for them.

Certain stock imagery © Thinkstock.
Any people depicted in stock imagery provided by Thinkstock are models, and such images are being used for illustrative purposes only.

ISBN: 978-1-4917-6006-2 (sc)
ISBN: 978-1-4917-6008-6 (hc)
ISBN: 978-1-4917-6007-9 (e)

Library of Congress Control Number: 2015901678

Print information available on the last page.

iUniverse rev. date: 4/13/2015

To Josh Pal, a life well lived

Acknowledgments

As always, thank you to the readers of *The Ethan Sparks Adventure Series*. To Britton Youngstrom for his inspiring character. To the patient women who typed the *Ethan Sparks* books to date: Sara Drake, Laura Berry, Deb Longhi, and Vickey Morales. Thanks to Deb Longhi for her help with the website. Also to Amy C. Bullock, Vince Holbrook, and all who have supported my quest to offer engaging stories that take young readers on adventures that both excite their imaginations and expand their worlds. It's been quite a ride—and one that isn't finished yet.

Prologue

I was home, minding my own business, just about to approach level eight on my new video game—when suddenly the doorbell insistently rang—and I was the only one home to answer it. I stomped to the door and threw it open. Before me, hulking in the doorway, stood two guys dressed in black suits. One was average height, compact, and low to the ground. The other was tall and beefy and had a huge, red splotch on his forehead that looked like he'd just banged his noggin Big Time on the doorframe.

"I'm Special Agent in Charge Lawrence," the compact one said. "This is my partner, Special Agent James."

James nodded, still rubbing the red bruise on his forehead.

"Secret Service?" I asked. "I suppose this is about vetting us because my father's been invited to a White House reception for the Terra Cotta soldier that China gave the US in his honor."

"No," Lawrence said. "We're FBI."

"May I see some ID please?"

Both agents held up their wallet shields.

"Is your mother home, son?" Agent James asked, cutting to the chase.

"As a matter of fact," I said, pointing to the driveway, "she's just arriving. Mom had to go out to get more peanut butter to make her famous PB&J cookies because my big, useless brother ate the entire seven-pound container of Jif that Mom just bought at Costco."

The two FBI agents turned and sighed as they watched my mom's Prius glide up the driveway, leaving its little carbon footprint. We waited for her to get out of the car with her grocery bag and walk up onto the front porch.

"Gentlemen," she politely insisted, "we have already been interviewed twice now. I assure you Ethan was only kidding when he said that he planned to shake the president's hand with one of those little electric buzzers in his palm."

"Mrs. Sparks," Agent Lawrence said, "may we please come in for a moment?"

"Why?" Mom said. "Something's wrong, isn't it?"

Lawrence swallowed a lump or something that must have suddenly appeared in his throat. He took in a deep breath, then addressed my mother with, "I'm sorry, Mrs. Sparks. I'm afraid I do have bad news for you."

"What!" my mother exclaimed. "Just tell me please."

"Please," Lawrence said, pointing to a couch and two chairs over on the wide part of the front porch, "may we sit down?"

Mom, clutching her grocery bag to her chest, went over and sat in one of the chairs. The two agents sat on the couch, and I stood behind my mother.

"All right, gentlemen," Mom said, "we're sitting." She paused. "Please, just tell us."

Lawrence nodded. "I'm afraid that Dr. Sparks has been kidnapped, along with his bodyguard and his entire archaeological team."

Suddenly, Mom let go of the grocery bag; eggs flew out of the carton and crashed onto the hardwood floor. I watched the yellow yolks run over the pine ... "Kidnapped," I repeated. "Are you sure?"

I looked up at the special agent in charge. "How come you know first? Why didn't the kidnappers contact us with the ransom demand?"

"The reason for this is odd," Lawrence admitted. "The kidnappers actually contacted the British government."

"The British government!" I yelled. "Why? What for?"

"Believe it or not," Lawrence told us, "the ransom demand is the Elgin Marbles."

"The Elgin Marbles!" I screamed in total disbelief. "The British Museum will never give up the Elgin Marbles! They probably wouldn't even do it for Prince William—maybe even Queen Elizabeth!"

"Yes," Lawrence agreed. "The British government has deemed this to be a terrorist demand, and like the United States, they have a strict policy never to negotiate with terrorists."

"Dad's dead," I muttered.

"No, Ethan," my mother shocked me by saying. "You have to Skype all of your previous spypartners—form a rescue team and get your father and his team back."

"Ah, Mrs. Sparks," James said, "that would be against protocol. The FBI has its own highly regulated protocol, which ensures a high conviction rate. I'm afraid that engaging civilians in this incident is impossible."

"No it isn't," the agent in charge said, "at least not in this case." He turned to me, "Ethan, we are aware of your special ops skills. Ah, Murphy, your father's bodyguard, briefed us after each of your previous five missions."

"Ethan," my mom said, obviously working hard to hold back her tears, "Murphy told your father and me that you're a natural at covert operations." She paused, turning to look me right in the eyes. "If you form a cohesive team with all your previous spypartners, I know that you will succeed in saving your dad and his team from certain death."

Then my mother turned to eyeball the FBI agents and added, "Gentlemen, I know that you both will assist my son and his friends. Isn't that correct?"

Agents Lawrence and James nodded like respectful, nice little boys.

"As you can see," I whispered to them, "my mom is really good at dealing with us guys."

Chapter 1

I, Ethan Ulysses Sparks, was on the most momentous mission of my life. This mission was so vital that I called in all of my previous spypartners to assist: my first spypartner, Chen-Jun, from China; Nico and Evangalia from our Greek adventure; Hakim from Egypt; Anya and Jack from our covert operation in the Mexican rain forest; and last but not least, Russell from our escapade in Britain. Everyone except for Russell was fourteen years old. Russell was seventeen.

Our current highly consequential mission was to save my father, Dr. Sparks, and his archaeological team from certain death. Which was why I was at the Raleigh International Airport waiting for their respective flights to arrive. I paid for everybody's airfare myself with most of the savings I'd earned working as a staff reporter for *The Young Explorer* magazine the past three years.

In the customs corral waiting for the international arrivals, I shuddered, knowing that the ransom demand that the kidnappers wanted would be something that even they had to know that they would never get. The British government—whether they considered this a terrorist demand or not—would without a doubt never give up the Elgin Marbles. They were one of the most priceless artifacts in the world—a collection of stone objects acquired by Lord Elgin in Athens between 1801 and 1812. Ancient Greek sculptures, inscriptions, and architectural features that were originally part of the Parthenon and other buildings on the Acropolis of ancient Athens.

Dad and his team, I thought, my blood turning cold, *face certain death. Mom said that my previous spypartners and I had to form a cohesive team and rescue them—failure is simply not an option.*

"E-than! E-than!" I suddenly heard.

I didn't have to look up to know that it was good old Chen-Jun from Xi'an, China, home of the Terra Cotta soldiers.

Too bad the kidnappers didn't just want a Terra Cotta soldier, I thought. *It would be a lot easier to get than the Elgin Marbles.*

"Chen-Jun! Chen-Jun!" I called out from the crowd, excitedly waving.

"No need to be polite with false exclamation," Chen-Jun said, dropping his backpack and duffel. He bowed his head affectionately. "I know that you are truly happy to see me again, but I also know that this unfortunately is not a happy reunion, my friend."

"Yeah." I nodded. *Wow*, I thought, *it's just like we saw each other yesterday.*

"Never could fool you," I admitted.

"No," I suddenly heard, "not like me."

I looked up, although I really didn't have to. I knew that voice well. Evangalia from Santorini, Greece. Nico lagged a bit behind her with his endearing, great big smile. With their help, we'd kept Poseidon's trident, or at least the Minoan artifact, from the clutches of a five-foot billionaire and his vicious spider monkey named Pou-Pou.

"Double-O-Seven," Nico said. "It is me, Double-O-Eight!"

"Yes," Evangalia threw in. "And me, the one"—index finger up to prove her point—"who saved both of your butts in my little, yellow rowboat."

Then she gave me the Greek spit-spit, *you're dead to me*, and added, "Your very first romantic kiss—remember?"

"No," I suddenly heard Anya say, "he doesn't remember." Anya's the girl I was currently Skype-dating because she lived in Mexico City, and I lived in Chapel Hill, North Carolina. "He forgot you entirely after *our* very first kiss."

I didn't know what to say or even how to respond to that. So I looked down at my shoes.

"*Aaaah-ooou*, Double-O-Seven," Nico abruptly whispered in my ear. "Evangalia is still very, very, very mad that you stopped Skype-dating her."

"Hey, dude." It was Jack's voice with his unmistakable California jargon. "Seems beatin' me and gettin' the babe back in that jungle in Mexico turned out to be a problem."

Then with a smirk, he added, "Remember, dude, I knew it would. I think I even tried to warn you, if I'm remembering correctly." He paused, his puka-shell necklace glinting at me. "And I am."

"Yes, yes," I then heard Hakim's distinct Egyptian accent agree. "Our friend here always gets into trouble."

"Absolutely correct." Last but not least, Russell's proper British-accent popped out of nowhere. "Ethan Sparks will indeed place you and himself in harm's way somehow." He faked clearing his throat and added, "I would imagine that for old man Sparks here, it is simply the siren call of an old habit."

Oh yeah, I thought, sighing, *the gang's all here, and it seems I have a reputation that they all concur with. Well, la-de-da.*

Besides, it's true, I thought, smirking. *I like taking people on adventures. So sue me.*

Once everyone had been cleared through customs, we headed out toward the van parked curbside. Climbing aboard, I spotted two goons in a black pickup truck watching us.

When all eight of us were seated and belted in, we took off. From the rearview mirror, I saw the black pickup truck pull away from the curb as well. It appeared to be following us. Glancing back several times, I saw that they were still tailing us—and that the windows had been tinted black.

I turned to Russell behind me. "Looks like we're being tailed," I told him.

He looked out the van's back window. "Are you referring to the black pickup truck?"

"Yeah."

"Do you think it could possibly be just paranoia?"

"No," I said, shrugging, "I don't think so."

The van stopped at a red light.

Suddenly, as if to prove my point, an explosion ripped out in a slow motion of fiery destruction, causing the rear end of the van to erupt into a fiery blaze and immediately produce an acrid smoke that stung our eyes and made it difficult to breathe.

Chapter 2

It took a few seconds for me to register the conscious realization that the rear end of the van had definitely erupted into a blaze of fire. When the acrid smoke started to make us cough, we instinctively kicked out the windows and jumped out of the van with our luggage.

Safely from the sidelines, we watched the van's tires burn and melt into black pools of liquid.

In a matter of minutes, ambulances, fire trucks, and police cars crowded the scene, forming a protective perimeter around us. I made sure that the authorities interviewed me first, immediately informing them that these were my friends from different countries and they'd been invited to North Carolina for a reunion. I made sure they also knew that my friends had my parents' consent to stay at our home, as well as their parents' permission. A cop went off to check that out while the other boys in blue interviewed the rest. Since my spypartners had previously read the dossier that I'd faxed them prior to joining this mission, they told the authorities the same and now cohesive cover story.

While the firemen trained their high-powered hoses and extinguished the van's tail-end blaze, Anya handed us all a wad of baby wipes to clean the soot off our faces and hands. Suddenly we heard one of the firemen yell out: "Hey, Captain, this is no accident! There's a timed incendiary device taped to the exhaust pipe—only there isn't nearly enough plastic to make a real difference. Also if the perps wanted to ensure maximum damage and no survival, they would have attached a great deal more of the explosive material to the gas tank itself." He paused. "I think the incident is intended to be a warning, a smoke bomb—nothing more."

"I think so too," I muttered under my breath, remembering the two goons following us in the black pickup truck with the tinted windows. "This is definitely a warning for us to back off."

"Yes," I heard Chen-Jun agree behind me, "a very dangerous warning. One we should not take lightly, my friend."

"And so it begins," I said, sighing. "You know, my friend," I confided in Chen-Jun, "ever since I found out that my father and his team had been kidnapped and were facing certain death without us rescuing them, I've been swimming in and out of myself."

"Of course." Chen-Jun explained, "It is classic shock, my friend."

Chapter 3

The replacement van that the Chapel Hill Police Department sent to transport the team home held only six comfortably. We were eight, so of course we had to cram ourselves in. To make matters worse, the AC didn't work. But what really made me uncomfortable was that I somehow found myself wedged between Anya and Evangalia. Also, believe it or not, I felt Evangalia elbowing me for more room.

Struggling to move, I reached into my backpack and started distributing new iPad Minis to everyone.

"Ah," Chen-Jun said, gratefully receiving his ops device, "you have given us the perfect tool to ensure this mission's quantitative certainty."

The others immediately agreed.

I looked out the van window, barely noticing the passing landscape. Everyone else navigated their new iPads with their custom-installed Global Internet Connection.

Soon, we were at number eight Zen Terrace, my humble 7,200-square-foot home. A renovated house originally built in 1865. I have the coolest attic bedroom in the world. It has a ton of space, six enormous windows, a zillion secret hiding places to conceal my spy equipment, a darkroom, and even my own bathroom.

Out on the front lawn stood Isabella Sparks, my mother, Carter Howard Sparks, my older brother, and Andrew Macallister, my best friend since Montessori. He has a photographic memory.

The van stopped. All eyes glanced up from their iPads.

"An enormous castle like this," Nico complained, "and you chose to sleep in the attic?"

"Yes, Nico," I said, "a gigantic attic—and the coolest Covert Ops Center in the whole world."

Chapter 4

Everyone assembled in my attic bedroom for a strategy meeting. There were a few things we needed to agree on before heading out on our mission. Also, my mother had *several ground rules that she felt compelled to share*. Her words.

"I think it is important to agree right from the start that we are a team, the sum of all eight parts," Anya insisted, starting the meeting. "Therefore, gender discrimination will not be tolerated. We must be a cohesive ops team to effectively carry out our extremely important mission."

Then Anya turned to Evangalia and said, "Right?"

"Absolutely," Evangalia concurred, nodding. "We are an equal team."

"All right," all the guys agreed, shrugging their shoulders.

Then everyone turned to me. "We are a cohesive team, right Ethan?" Anya pointedly asked me. "All *equal* partners that will work toward our one objective: rescuing Dr. Sparks and his archaeological team."

"Agreed," I said. "However, as you will all also agree, we need a Lead. Given my experience, I volunteer to take on that role."

"No thank you," Anya said. "I think that being one in the sum of eight parts, we should each bring to the team a particular skill that we most excel at."

"I totally concur," Chen-Jun said. "We will be much stronger as a team if we singularly focus on our most accomplished skill."

"Okay," I agreed, shrugging. "Then let's say my most accomplished skill is being the Lead."

"Perhaps," Russell said in his proper British accent. "However, Sparks, another of your most accomplished skills, at least in my opinion, is lip reading."

"No," I argued, "I think it's my gut feelings that really drive the missions we're on—again, the reason why I should be Lead."

"I tell you what," my mother, Isabella Sparks, interjected with that finality that I know so well. "Collaboration is what makes a team perform more successfully. As Anya pointed out, everyone should bring to the table whatever their signature skill is. Although as opposed to just focusing on only one particular strength, I suggest you all just instinctively let the process unfold; allow all of your accomplished skills to work together and drive you as a team toward one common goal—that of course being to bring my husband and his team safely home."

"I thoroughly agree!" Hakim exclaimed with his Egyptian sensibility.

"As do I," Chen-Jun added.

"Sounds like a plan to me," Layback Jack said.

"Yes," Russell agreed, "the strategy is indeed most sound."

"I have said it before," Nico said, index finger up, "and I will say it again: *a mother is a font of wisdom.*"

"I know that my mother definitely is," Anya agreed.

"Yes." Evangalia nodded knowingly. "A mother is like baklava—layer upon layer of goodness."

"Oh yeah," I agreed, "I do believe we have established a team—now let's get out there and start our mission."

"Good," my mother, Isabella Sparks, said, "because I am depending solely on the eight of you. Now, before you all start your mission, how about some milk and cookies?" She held out a tray of her famous snickerdoodles.

"Yeah, and I'm the milk guy," my big brother added, handing out little cartons with straws in them. *I'm sure the elementary-school milk cartons were his idea. He's being condescending, as always, by pointing out that we're still kids because he's three years older than us.*

All the fourteen-year-olds and seventeen-year-old Russell took their milk cartons off the tray, cookies in hand. Then I heard my best friend, Drew, whisper in my ear, "Ethan, I need to talk to you privately in the secret Bat Cave."

"Okay," I said, following him down the hall into my walk-in closet.

Once in the Bat Cave, I turned to him and said, "Let me guess, you want in on this mission."

Drew nodded. "Yes."

"I already thought you were." I lowered my voice. "When I learned of the kidnapping, you were the first one I went to, remember?" I looked him right in the eye and added, "Our objective here is to rescue my dad and his team from certain death. And I wouldn't even think about going on this mission without you."

"Well," my mom said, startling us, "so glad that you two boys sorted that out. We all know what a valuable asset that Drew is." Then she gave us the *mom eye*, as I call it.

"Don't worry, Mom," I promised her, "we'll get them all back safely."

"I believe in you, Ethan. I always have. Murphy has told me what a great operative you are. That you have a real talent for this sort of thing, as well as your previous spypartners."

I nodded.

"This is why I agreed to let you and your spypartners go on this dangerous mission." She paused. "That's why I called all their parents and asked them to agree to this as well." Another dramatic Mom pause. "It's also why I'm not dwelling on the fact that someone planted a ridiculous smoke bomb on your airport transport van to warn you off."

Someone behind me cleared his throat.

I turned, and there stood my big brother, Carter. "Ethan," he said, actually hugging me, "I know that you and your spyguys will bring Dad and his team back safely."

All I could do was nod. *Wow*, I thought, *who are you and what have you done with my brother?*

Chapter 5

It was obvious to start in my dad's office. He's the director of the Research Laboratories of Archaeology at the University of North Carolina at Chapel Hill. Our duffels were still loaded in the van, which was ready to take us to the airport the moment we ascertained where we should start our mission.

Now all my eight spypartners—correction, Team Eclipse, as we decided to call ourselves—thoroughly searched every nook and cranny in my dad's cluttered office for even a whiff of a clue.

The first clue turned out to be discovered by me. I found a cryptic e-mail sent to my dad's office computer via his smartphone the day after he'd been kidnapped. The e-mail seemed to be a set of coordinates. Underneath them were a set of numbers and the words: *We are being*—then the communication just stopped.

"My guess," I told everyone, "is Dad's kidnappers discovered him composing that e-mail on his phone and confiscated it before he managed to finish the communication. At least he managed to send a partial message."

I kept to myself the thought that my father had sent this e-mail clue to his office computer because it was the only e-mail address he could remember. Dad can be such an oxymoron; he can remember the carbon dates of artifacts from the Neolithic Period, but he can't remember e-mail addresses or phone numbers.

"Hey, guys!" I called out. "Look at this. The set of numbers appears to be coordinates, and my dad sent this e-mail the day *after* he was kidnapped."

Anya got there first. She whipped out her iPad. Moments later, we heard, "These coordinates pinpoint a location in the Peruvian rain forest."

"Yes," Chen-Jun immediately concurred, looking down at his iPad. "These are definitely Peruvian rain forest coordinates, specifically the part of the jungle in Machu Picchu that borders Brazil."

"Yes, definitely on the Brazilian border," Hakim confirmed.

"Well, Team Eclipse," I said, "it's off to Peru."

"And the first flight that leaves is in three hours and twenty-six minutes," Anya said, staring down at her iPad.

"Well," Evangalia reminded us, "how perfect—there's a van waiting outside to take us to the airport."

"Very convenient," Nico said, with his signature sarcastic grin.

"I found a handwritten note that I believe Dr. Sparks wrote," Chen-Jun said. "It is very difficult to read."

He handed me the note. "Yes," I confirmed. "This is definitely Dad's scrawl. It says, *I believe that I am being followed by two goons. I have a bad feeling about this.*"

I looked up. "*Goons*," I said. "Two goons in a black pickup truck with tinted windows and access to bomb material."

Chapter 6

The red eye to Cuzco, Peru, from JFK proved lucky. We were all sitting together in the back of the jet. The last two rows in fact. So different from our connecting flight from Charlotte when most of us had to be scattered throughout the plane.

However, with the victors came the spoils, because I was uncomfortably sandwiched between Anya and Evangalia in our *cozy* little three-seat row. Describing how awkward I felt would be like dancing without music.

While everyone slept, Nico snoring and Hakim talking in his sleep about some new high-tech spy equipment that he'd brought, I went over all the Intel I had so far.

The FBI had knocked on our front door at number eight Zen Terrace to inform us that dad and his archaeological team were being held for ransom—kidnapped.

Less than twenty-four hours later, Team Eclipse jumped onto a plane headed for Cuzco, Peru, the Inca capital.

According to the itinerary that Anya had quickly booked on her iPad, after landing in Cuzco, we would take a train to Aguas Calientes, then a bus from Aguas Calientes to Machu Picchu.

There we would meet our tour guide, a one-man operation owned and operated by a guy named Britton Yangstrum. When I Googled him, I found out that he was a nineteen-year-old Aussie and that he'd gotten over his fear of heights by climbing Mount Everest.

Good, I thought, *I like Aussies.*

Britton would then take all nine of us to the exact coordinates listed in Dad's last e-mail.

No, I quickly told myself. *Not his last!*

I yawned—more of a stress yawn than a tired one. In fact, I was wired. Still, I knew that this red-eye flight would be my only chance to grab some sleep.

We all had an airplane pillow and blanket. So I snuggled in and deliberately left an equal distance between myself, Evangalia, and Anya.

If I know California Jack, and I do, he had taken a melatonin to grab some Zs.

Chen-Jun was ruminating because he was only half in REM. He truly wanted to rescue my dad. So did Drew, Nico, Hakim, and Russell. But they were smart enough to get the necessary shut-eye on this flight while they could.

I better get some sleep myself, I realized. *In the morning, we're going to hit the ground running.*

This mission will succeed. It will. It has to. Failure is not an option.

Chapter 7

The pilot abruptly made the announcement that we were about to make our final descent. It woke us up as if it were an alarm clock.

"So now it's a train from Cuzco, Peru, to Aguas Calientes," Anya announced.

"Then a bus from Aguas Calientes to Machu Picchu," I said, taking over the briefing.

"Where we will meet Britton Yangstrum," Anya volleyed, seizing it right back. "Britton will take us to the exact coordinates Dr. Sparks listed in his e-mail communication."

"Yeah," I slid in, "a location in the Peruvian rain forest, pretty darn close to the equator."

"Yes," Anya confirmed, vying for control. "Those coordinates are indeed close to the equator."

"Yes *indeed*," Russell said sarcastically from across the aisle. "Quite close."

"And let's not forget we will be in the rain forest," Evangalia said. "A rain forest sounds *so* pretty."

I turned to Evangalia. "The rain forest isn't as romantic as you may think," I told her.

"I categorically disagree," Anya suddenly whispered in my ear. "I found our little rain forest adventure to be quite romantic."

I just sighed.

"Ah," I heard Drew, my oldest friend, whisper in my good ear, "seems ego may turn out to be a problem after all."

"Not as long as we let Anya run the ops," I told him.

"I heard that," Anya said. "And look who's talking!"

"Ah," I reminded her, "I believe you recently said that for us to succeed in our objective, we should operate as a cohesive team?" I paused. "Well I suggest that in order to do so, we all bring to the table our special skills and lead only when we are employing said skills."

"Si," Anya pointed out, "and one of my many special skills is managing the travel itinerary and briefing the team on its schedule." She paused, hand on hip. "I believe that is exactly what I was attempting to do while you kept trying to take the itinerary brief over."

She looked me right in the eye, actually daring me to say another word.

"Oh," I said, just to get in the last word.

Chapter 8

The train to Aguas Calientes turned out to be super cool. Retro cool. Lots of wood—old-fashioned woodwork actually. Definitely a quirky, old train chugging its way from Cuzco, the Inca capital of Peru, to Aguas Calientes, the closest rail stop to the outpost of Machu Picchu.

Earlier, Anya had shown me some Internet photos of Aguas Calientes. Basically, it could boast being a small town with a bus station that will take you to Machu Picchu.

Usually the *clickety-clack* of old trains on rutted rails soothed me, but not this time. I suddenly got a queasy feeling in my stomach, and my hands and forehead started dripping with cold sweat. Then out of the blue, these terrible stabs of anxiety sliced through me, cutting me to the bone.

Please, please, I silently pleaded, closing my eyes. *Please let them be safe and sound in the rain forest.* Then suddenly my imagination saw a pressure cooker on a gas stove, its little, circular top violently steaming and shrieking—then *boom*! The little top exploded!

Abruptly, a fog seized my brain, rendering it useless. I actually struggled to stay focused in my head. Again, I felt like I was a piece of driftwood swimming in and out of myself, easily getting fatigued and starting to be pulled under and drowned. This made me begin to panic and caused my heart to drill through my chest. My breathing hyperventilated, and I became so dizzy that I started to pass out.

"Ethan, are you okay?" I heard my best friend, Drew, say in my good ear. "You're hyperventilating, my friend."

"No, I'm not!" I insisted. "I'm just cogitating on the notion of inconclusiveness."

"Yes indeed," Russell said. "Well, stop doing that, please. You must remain calm, Ethan. You must."

I did the head left-to-right swivel and said to them both. "Okay, guys, I will."

They both looked at me like they didn't believe me.

"I'm fine!" I lied.

"Ethan," Hakim said, "this mission is extremely personal to you. Feeling acute anxiety like this is quite normal, my friend."

"Si," Anya added, "if someone pushed my mama into danger, I would be loco with worry. We will help you through this, *miho*. You will see; all will be well."

"Yes, *dear, dear* Ethan," Evangalia said, taking my hand and squeezing it. "We will safely rescue your beloved papa and his loyal team."

"There is absolutely, positively no doubt about this!" Nico exclaimed, hand up like a mighty sword.

"We will succeed in our objective. I am most sure of this," Chen-Jun said in an undisputable tone.

"You know, dude," Jack tossed in, "even though we all know that this mission is going to succeed, it's okay to have a panic attack. Actually, it's normal." He paused, and the bright white puka shells around his neck glinted. "But I'll tell you, dude, the way to get over a panic attack is to acknowledge it and see it for what it is."

"Umm," I said, "let me guess—fear."

"Yup," he said, nodding. "And I say feel the fear but don't let it run you. Instead, you control it with all viable resources and options available to you; in this case, all of us."

"Thanks, Jack," I said.

"No sweat, man."

No one said another word about the subject. Instead, we manufactured some small talk as the train clickety-clacked along the old, scarred rails. Soon the thick border of trees on both sides thinned into the beginnings of a small town.

Silently, a bit tired even, we exited the train and trudged over to the bus station. The station had one bus—an old, decrepit, dusty bus from the fifties or sixties. Once our duffels and backpacks were stowed and we were sitting on cracked leather seats, the old bus started up with a foul-smelling belch and farted its way to Machu Picchu.

Chapter 9

The old bus definitely smelled like goat, and it had a rooftop loaded with all our backpacks and duffel bags, which had me worried that a bag or two might fall off whenever the bus hit a pothole in the dusty dirt road. The springs in my seat were shot; one of them even poked me in the thigh. However, everyone had their noses buried in their iPads, and I became grateful for the quiet.

Looking out the window, I started seeing definite signs that we were approaching a rain forest in Peru. The dense trees were much taller and skinnier than the ones back in town.

"Yes," Drew said, next to me, "you can definitely tell we're getting close to a rain forest."

"Drew," I said, *not* turning to him, "I have to tell you, this mission really does have me, well, very *anxious*."

"I know," Drew said. "Me too. And I have to tell you, Ethan, I became really worried when you had that panic attack on the train."

"Um," I realized out loud, "I guess I really did have a panic attack."

"You were gasping for breath, Ethan. It looked like you were drowning."

"Well, that's definitely the way I felt."

I turned to my best friend, a friend that I had played spy with since we were five years old. "I meant it when I said that I couldn't do this without you."

"We're going to get them back, Ethan!" He paused. "We are."

"I know," I said. "We have to." I turned to him. "Remember, failure is *never* an option."

"Of course I remember that," Drew said. "It used to be our mantra."

"Still is," I insisted. "*Still is.*"

"You know, Ethan," Drew said, "Jack made a very good point; we can control our anxiety by approaching this mission scientifically, by employing all of our viable options and effectively utilizing all of our resources."

"I know," I told him, "but ..." I lowered my voice to confide something only to him. "Well, to be honest with you, my anxiety isn't really the fear of failing in this mission." I paused. "It's, um, well, it's a sudden realization of how much I love my dad. And, um, how much I'd miss him if he were gone despite how he annoys the crap out of me."

"I understand," Drew said, nodding. "I feel the same way about my dad."

I turned to my best friend and sighed. "Well since we're being so touchy-feely here," I added, "I guess these love-your-family sentiments would have to include my mother and even Carter, my arrogant, conceited, older brother."

"Yup," Drew concurred, "family's family, I guess."

"Yeah," I agreed, shrugging, "I guess."

Chapter 10

The bus from Aguas Calientes to Machu Picchu arrived pretty much on time. Out of my window, I saw Britton Yangstrum. He stood tall, had those outdoor-working-type muscles, and emanated a relaxed openness with his friendly facial expressions and sincere-lookin' smile. There he stood, dressed in khakis, a brown leather vest, a bush hat that strapped under his neck, and boots, leaning confidently on the side of his twelve-passenger van with the words *Yangstrum Adventures* painted boldly on its side. He had hair like mine—short, spiked-up, jet-black. A good look, if you ask me.

This guy Britton definitely seems the right man for the job, I thought. *Those muscular guns of his will have no problem hacking the way into the jungle. Hopefully when I'm his age, I'll have guns like that.*

We exited the bus. Anya went right over to Britton and introduced herself as the one who'd hired him to take us into the rain forest. It could have been my imagination, but I got the feeling Anya was flirting with him. It totally surprised me that this didn't bother me.

"G'day, all," Britton said, taking his bush hat off and nodding at us. Then he took our duffel bags one by one and easily secured them on top of the van. Again, it surprised me when he started flirting right back at her and that didn't upset me either.

Funny thing, I realized. *I, um, actually feel, well, relieved.*

I looked over at Evangalia. It seemed that she realized it too. At least her old, familiar, sweet smile conveyed that. I had to admit it, I missed that smile. I hadn't seen it since we broke up.

We boarded the van, and I noticed Anya sit up front near Britton. Now I wondered if she had decided to deliberately try to make me jealous. You know, to get a reaction out of me. Some assurance that I still wanted to date her or a definitive confirmation that I didn't.

I took the back seat next to Nico.

"Hello, Double-O-Seven," Nico said, smiling. "Are you okay, my friend?"

"I have to be," I answered, sighing. "You know the expression, failure is not an option?"

"Yes." Nico nodded. "But this is not what I meant. It seems to me that Anya is flirting with the new muscle guy and that this is not bothering you. So, are you liking Evangalia again?" He turned to me. "You know what I mean by this?"

"Oh yeah," I said. "I know exactly what you mean. But don't worry, my friend. Evangalia told me that you two were promised." I put my hands up, indicating hands off.

"Evangalia no tell the truth. I think she say this because she likes you again too and wants to make you jealous."

"Hah ... good to know ... but I can't think about that now."

"Yes, my friend, you must rescue your father and his faithful team. Thinking of this will only be a distraction."

"Umm, yes, a distraction ... we must stay focused on the mission," I agreed, nodding.

The *Yangstrum Adventures* van roared to life. Its powerful engine seemed to concur that being focused was the immediate thing to do.

As the van with its oversized tires held its own on the rutted dirt road with huge craterlike potholes, I looked out my dirt-streaked window and saw trees so tall that they'd bent over and their tops had knitted together to form a canopy that blocked out the sun and made the crazy-hot temperature outside become almost bearable.

Ten minutes after meeting Britton Yangstrum, he and his humorous take on life became a part of Team Eclipse. We even knew the nickname his *mates* back home called him: Ying-Yang. An odd name for an Aussie, but it fit him.

For some reason, I suddenly felt hope. I guess everybody else did too, because a mutual, relaxed conversation sprung up and soon created a good mood that invigorated us. Truth be told, the *hope* we felt seemed to be entirely predicated upon one thing—that my father and his team would be at the exact coordinates that we were heading for when we arrived to rescue them.

Chapter 11

Less than an hour later, Team Eclipse boldly stood at the threshold to the rain forest. Actually, it was an overgrown wall of jungle brush reinforced with thick, twisted vines—oh, about ten, twelve feet tall. Each of us strapped the miniature high-powered flashlights to our forehead that I'd purchased on spytools.com.

Britton Yangstrum stood six feet, two inches. My guess, he was two hundred pounds—solid, sturdy, *dependable* pounds. The kind of muscular pounds with big forearms that you knew would get you to the necessary coordinates in the Peruvian rain forest. And with a mean-lookin' machete in hand, he immediately started whacking the jungle growth into pulverized shreds to provide us with a path. His leadership proved itself immediately and inspired confidence.

Oh yeah, I thought, following right behind him, *Team Eclipse definitely has a capable guide.*

There were ten of us now. Together, we would rescue my dad

and his eight-member loyal team: five archaeology guys and one woman who turned out to be a whiz at mapping the dig grids; Dad's body guard named Murphy, one of my good friends; and the guy who taught me photography, another good friend named Rolf, the team's official photographer.

Rolf's wife, Dr. Sarum, was going to have their first baby, twins actually—a girl they were going to name Rowina and a boy they were going to name Ethan. If I'm remembering correctly, the babies were due to be born in three weeks and two days. Rolf planned to be there. He would be.

"E-than," I heard Chen-Jun say behind me. "It seems you are feeling some hope now."

"Yes," I said. "I definitely am."

"I am as well," Hakim said, next in line.

"Yes! Yes!" Nico said, excitedly entering the conversation. "This is true—so very, very true. I very much feel hope now too!"

"Good," Anya proclaimed. "It is important to harness the power of positive thinking."

"Anya's right," Jack slipped in. "And if we all harness it, it will become a power to the tenth degree."

"Quite right," Russell agreed. "There of course have been definitive studies proving this."

"One does not need a scientific study to know this," Evangalia argued. "You just simply have to feel it to know that it is true."

"I'm with Evangalia on this one," Britton said, joining right in. "However, I must admit I do see the penetrating power in positive thought as well, especially if it's a group thinkin' it all at the same time."

"So," Drew said, his usual pragmatic self, "let's all project hope together."

"All right," I agreed, "let's."

As if on cue, a stream of bright sunlight penetrated through a hole in the thick canopy of treetops that soared overhead. Then a little spider monkey swooped down out of nowhere and bopped me on the head. He must have been quite amused because he shrieked with laughter and stole the high-powered flashlight strapped to my forehead.

Chapter 12

"Hey, Britton," I called out, walking behind him as he vigorously thrashed and slashed a clear path through the tangle of twisted jungle bush with his machete. "If you're getting tired, I'd be happy to work the machete for a while."

"Thanks, mate," he said, sounding appreciative. "But I'm just fine and dandy."

"All right." I nodded. "Then do you mind answering a personal question?" I asked, digging into my backpack for a replacement forehead flashlight.

"Curious about something, eh?"

"Oh yeah," I answered.

"Well then ask away, mate. Ask away."

"How did you get to own a Machu Picchu adventure company?" I asked. "Why didn't you establish one in Australia where you come from? Lots of adventure Down Under, especially in the Outback."

"Sense of humor, I guess," Britton said, shrugging. "Almost everyone back home has one. It seemed more important to me to stand out, be an expat and all that."

I nodded my head. "Yeah, I get it."

"Thought you might, mate," he said. "I pegged you as a world wanderer the moment I laid eyes on ya."

"Uh," I told him, "I pegged you as a wanderer the moment I met you too. Also, well, shall we say, I think, based on an immediate first impression, that you're always open to raising the bar on your adventure seeking."

"Well, you're right," he said, without hesitation. "As open as a clam actually."

"Good," I said, nodding. "Then how about joining our mission? Team Eclipse could use a good man like you."

"Fine with me, mate," Britton said, without even thinking about it. "So happens that I have always wanted to be a spy. I've actually dreamt about it since I was knee high to a grasshopper."

"I thought so," I told him.

Britton stopped hacking his way through the jungle for a moment. He turned to me and with a wink said, "Takes one to know one, eh?"

"Oh yeah," I said, "you've got that right."

"Kindred spirits, I imagine."

"Absolutely," I agreed.

"Gotta say," Britton said, looking down at his compass to make sure that we were heading toward the right coordinates, "sounds like a bloomin' adventure to me." He paused, turned, looked me right in the eye, and added, "But I want to assure you, mate, I know this is no recreational adventure. No, sir, it's much more than that. In fact, it's a matter of life or death with your dad and all."

I nodded. Britton's index finger saluted me in silent solidarity. With that, he turned and soldiered on.

"Uh," I said, "I have another question."

"Shoot, mate!" he exclaimed, whacking the jungle bush into smithereens. "I understand curiosity all too well."

"I noticed that you have a little, scarred, brown leather journal sticking out of your shirt's front pocket. Do you keep notes on all your adventures?"

"I do," he said, "but my old, scarred notebook is also for doodlin'. I've been, well, doodling all of my life. I guess you can say that I'm a habitual doodler. Me dad's a therapist, the shrink kind, he says my doodlin' is my way of grasping onto the present moment because it makes me actually stop moving and take the time to sit and doodle my thoughts instead of just racing adventurously through my life."

"Wow," I said, "that's so cool. And very ying-yang balanced if you think about it."

"Hey, mate!" he said, sounding impressed with my observation. "Perhaps that's the cosmic reason that I really got the nick name Ying-Yang, and not just because it's a play on my last name, Yangstrum!"

"Boy," I said, looking up. "I love the way that life has its hidden meanings and textures."

Overhead, the canopy of trees thinned out and started to give way to a torrent of hazy, almost surreal light. Colorful birds were chatting in the now sparse tree limbs, and they looked brilliant against the lush tropical greenness. Then suddenly the squawks from these colorful birds were drowned out by the blood-curdling roar of a group of howler monkeys passing by overhead, jumping long sprints to the thickets of trees off to the left.

It may have been my imagination, but I felt the pull of the equator. Imagination or not, the tug kept me moving toward the hazy, streaming light up ahead.

"Only fifty feet or so left to go," Britton told me, "and we'll be there. Just like I thought, the exact coordinates you e-mailed me are definitely an enormous clearing. Big enough to even land a bush copter."

"Also, in my research I learned," Britton continued, "that there's even a little waterfall there. Well, more of a spit really."

As we entered the clearing, it shocked me to see the two FBI agents who had informed us that Dad and his team had been kidnapped standing in front of that waterfall.

Chapter 13

Anya had e-mailed Britton the exact coordinates that now took us to the remote corner of the Peruvian rain forest that touched the Brazilian border. Obviously Special Agent in Charge Lawrence and his partner, Special Agent James, had intercepted that e-mail and beat us here by taking a bush copter to the location. Searching the surrounding perimeter with my field glasses, I saw the small, two-passenger, unmarked, camouflaged helicopter inconspicuously stashed in a thicket of brush.

"Hello, Special Agent in Charge Lawrence and Special Agent James," I said, hand out to shake theirs as I walked up to them.

"Hello, Ethan," Agent Lawrence said, shaking my hand firmly, with authority but not with brute force like Agent James did.

"I am sorry to have to tell you this," Lawrence said. "Your father and his team are no longer here."

"Yes, sir," I said. "But I feel in my gut that they were here."

"Me too," Lawrence said, nodding. "Especially since your

father e-mailed these coordinates to his office nineteen hours *after* his kidnapping." He paused. "Good job finding the coordinates before we did, Ethan."

"You guys still beat us here," I said, trying not to be a spoilsport.

"Ethan," Lawrence said seriously, "we're on the same team, are we not? Our objective to rescue your father and his team is mutual. Therefore, the more resources to realize that objective successfully, the better. Wouldn't you agree?"

"Definitely," I said, totally agreeing. "And my team is fortunate to join forces with yours, especially since you and James carry guns."

"Conversely," Lawrence said, sounding sincere, "we are also fortunate to have the resources that you and your team bring to the table."

"Thanks," I said, accepting the compliment.

"Now," the agent in charge said, "back to business. Of course you are aware that this makes this area a crime scene."

"Yes," I sighed, nodding. "I am aware of this."

"And I imagine that all twelve of us will be working it?" Agent Lawrence asked.

"Yes, Special Agent Lawrence," I answered. "All twelve of us will definitely be working it."

"That's irregular," Special Agent James sliced in. "Incorrect protocol, actually."

"Oh yeah?" I said to the big galoof. "You wouldn't even have found the crime scene if we hadn't led you to it."

"That's partially correct," Agent Lawrence acknowledged.

"However, Agent James is right; civilians working a crime scene is indeed highly irregular."

"Still," I insisted, "we're all working the crime scene together despite protocol. Isn't that correct, Agent Lawrence?"

"Yes," the FBI man answered. "We are in total agreement regarding this change in department protocol." He paused. "As I mentioned Ethan, the Bureau is aware of your reputation as a skillful, independent field operative."

"Great," I said, looking up at the vast, open overhead and seeing the sun dramatically setting with bright red slashes across the sky. "Then you know how much help we can be."

Both FBI men just nodded.

"Good," I said, "because I know that my father left me a visual clue somewhere around here to tell me where the kidnappers were taking them next."

"Then it's fortuitous that you're here to find it, Ethan," Lawrence said. "Because for us, you see, the trail has gone cold."

I kept to myself the fear that that might happen to me as well.

Chapter 14

We immediately started working the crime scene. Agent Lawrence assigned us our specific quadrants to work, and we went right to it, high-powered flashlights strapped to our foreheads. Thankfully I had packed a spare, because you never know when a monkey is going to swoop down and steal yours on a trek in the rain forest.

Agent James's smile flickered on and off as if it had a loose connection, you know, like it had bad wiring or something. My guess, James barely managed to contain the fact that he was totally irritated by the entire situation. It obviously proved to be too messy for him, not the usual protocol, not the way the FBI or he normally did things at a crime scene. The way he'd been taught.

Thankfully, his partner, Lawrence, proved more flexible. Actually, Lawrence seemed to be even *more* than flexible; he appeared to be open to our search methods, even showing admiration for our thoroughness. *Oh yeah*, I thought, *he's glad that we're helping. More sets of eyes—and trained, skilled ones at that.*

Both FBI agents stood out in their black suits in the rain forest. The compact, low-to-the-ground Agent Lawrence didn't sweat, but the beefy Agent James did. Lawrence treated us with professional courtesy, respect even. James just walked around grumping, either muttering to himself or yelling at one of us if he thought we were contaminating the crime scene, which, admittedly, we may have been doing, at least according to the official FBI evidence-collection protocol.

"Over here!" Drew suddenly called out. We all rushed over to the quadrant that Drew had been assigned to work.

Soon we were looking at the visual clue that I had hoped for. Three words carved into the back of a tree in my dad's distinctive scrawl. The words were: *Brazilian Exports, Limited.*

Anyone but my dad would have abbreviated the word *Limited* with LTD.

We also found Dad's smartphone about six feet in front of the tree. It had been violently smashed into three pieces. From the way the three pieces had flown and scattered, it appeared as if they'd been thrown in brute, goon-like anger.

"Brazilian Exports Limited," Chen-Jun said, looking down at his global smartphone, "is in Rio de Janeiro."

"Next stop," I turned to Lawrence and said, "Rio de Janeiro."

"Yes," Lawrence said, affirmatively. "It wouldn't surprise me if Brazilian Exports is a ghost company."

"Yeah," I sighed. "And I hope my dad and his team are alive and well there."

Chapter 15

Drew and I sipped coffee at an Internet café in downtown Cuzco. The rest of Team Eclipse relaxed at the two-story hotel at the end of the block. While they washed up, my old friend searched for the next flight to Rio.

Since the bush copter that had transported the FBI agents to the rain forest held only two passengers, Lawrence had to call for a larger helicopter to take us back to the Yangstrum Adventures van. Then our new team member, Britton, had sped us as fast as he could to the city of Cuzco. Lawrence and James had already left for Rio in a private FBI jet. Evidently, working with the local bureau office, they had some diplomatic protocol and red tape to cut through so that we would not be arrested for breaking and entering once we arrived and conducted our surveillance of the building known as Brazilian Exports, Ltd.

"The earliest flight to Rio leaves in three hours and ten minutes from Cuzco," Drew informed me. He paused, scrolling his iPad over to the airlines' reservation site. "And there's plenty of seating still available."

"Good," I said, sipping my coffee now that it had finally cooled down enough not to burn my mouth. "Three hours until take off. We have plenty of time."

"Actually, we don't," he corrected me, sending an urgent text to all the team members. "Building in how long it will take the ten of us to get to the airport, as well as the fact that we're required to be at the airport two hours before flight time, I'd say that you have two minutes or so to finish your coffee so we can get the others and start the transportation process."

I looked at him. Same intense brown eyes, same shaggy mop of blond-colored straw for hair. But now at fourteen, he'd already grown to be six feet tall and 140 pounds of intellect and attitude. An attitude I might add that he sometimes flaunted because he and his photographic memory were accurate and well informed most of the time. Some would say that Drew was a know-it-all.

Yeah, I thought, *me for one.*

"I know you think that I'm a know-it-all," Drew said, like he'd been reading my mind. "But out in the field, that could be an asset. Wouldn't you agree?"

"I see your exercises in making your mind more telepathic are working," I said.

"Yes," Drew admitted. "They are. They definitely are." He paused, giving me the annoying all-knowing eye. "Either that or you're just predictable."

One by one, the texts from the others came in. Everyone was ready to go.

Chapter 16

Out our van windows, I saw the sinister night lights that revealed the infamous city known as Rio. It seemed to still be the same living and breathing city that I remembered from when I'd been there with my family on vacation. Very live and let live. Rio is the capital of Brazil and an enormous seaport.

Enormous seaport cities are always diverse and filled with ex-pats from other countries, and Rio is definitely one of them.

When I turned twelve, we went there on a family vacation. Whenever Dad managed to get time off in between digs or teaching at UNC, and Mom had finished researching a cookbook or taping a season of shows for the Cooking Network, and Carter had a break from training or performing in a track meet—we went on some great family vacations. Places like Tahiti, the Great Barrier Reef in Australia, Costa Rica, the Panama Canal, India, and Thailand to name a few.

Murphy, an ex-CIA spook and my dad's bodyguard, always

joined the family on these vacations. Boy, I remember Murphy being a lot more on red alert here in Rio than on most of the previous family vacations.

You know, the older I get, I thought, *the more I realize how much I love my family. Even Murphy.*

The twelve-passenger airport van stopped. Since there were only ten of us, the room for twelve made our trip very comfortable, even with our duffels and backpacks. I have to say, Anya did a great job with our transportation itinerary. She'd even found Britton, now an asset to the team.

The van stopped in front of an old, redbrick building at the end of a row of old, redbrick buildings. A tall, skinny, ten-story hovel on a corner with an alley.

"This is the correct address according to my GPS," Chen-Jun said, checking his iPad.

"Mine as well," Hakim said, confirming said position on his device as well.

"No doubt a front as you Yanks say," Russell pointed out.

"Yeah, dude," Jack said sarcastically, "no doubt."

"It's the money holder all right," Britton kicked in. "You know, mates, the bank."

"I think you mean money launderer," Drew clarified.

"A bigger company than I expected," Evangalia said.

I turned to Evangalia. "Don't worry; you're safe," I assured her. "You're a member of an elite ops team."

"Yes, I know," Evangalia told me, with a sarcastic twist in the corner of her mouth. "I too am elite. Do you not agree?"

"And how," I said. "You are definitely *elite*."

Evangalia smiled.

Behind me in the next to the last row of the van, I felt Anya's glare on my back.

"Hey, Double-O-Seven," Nico whispered in my ear. "How you say in English? Oh yes, *if looks could kill, you would be dead.*"

Chapter 17

"Luckily it's the dead of night and all of the employees have gone home for the day," I said as we scoped out the perimeter of the building.

"It's odd, don't you think, mate?" Britton turned to me and said, "No security guards."

"Yeah," I agreed, "it is."

So I reached into my backpack and took out my pair of night-vision goggles. Intently searching the surrounding area, I came upon a greenish-tinted Lawrence and James skulking in the doorway of the building across the street. Lawrence nodded to me and then mouthed, *We couldn't get a search warrant, but we've got your back if you get caught.* Then James mouthed, *But don't get caught*! Russell was right, I am good at lip reading. All my practice was proving that.

"A little spooky, no?" I heard Nico ask, sounding unnerved. "You don't think there are big, mean dogs inside?"

"Only one way to find out," I said, pointing to what appeared to be a basement window in the back of the building, hidden in the shadows of the alley. "Let's go in and find out."

I finally pried open the window and easily squeezed myself through it and down into the basement feetfirst. Unfortunately, Nico had predicted correctly; before us, growling, teeth bared, fangs dripping yellow saliva that glistened in the darkness, stood a guard dog, a pit bull, no less. Before I knew it, the ferocious dog leapt for my jugular.

Then out of nowhere, Britton knocked me clear out of the way and used his belt like a lion tamer employs as a training whip.

The guard dog immediately backed off, and with whip in hand, the Aussie forced the growling pit bull into an enormous shipping crate. Then he slammed the hinged door to the wood crate shut, locked it securely with its attached latch, and calmly put his belt back through the loops in his khaki pants.

"Thanks," I managed to say, the adrenalin still coursing through me.

"You're welcome, mate," he said, with a great big smile.

Soon, the others joined us in the basement, slipping through the casement window one by one. An immediate chatter broke out about what had just happened, along with a great deal of sincere *good job* slaps on the back from the guys for our hero Britton. The girls hugged him. I have to admit, I felt so grateful that I wanted to hug him too; but instead we just fistbumped.

Evangalia started looking through a tool chest on a nearby worktable and pulled out a manual drill. Then she began drilling breathing holes in the enormous wood crate, totally unfazed by the big, growling dog trying to get at her from inside.

The rest of us checked out the rows and rows of the other shipping crates. A lot were empty. Some had those cheesy strung beads and feathers that the people who attend the carnival in Rio use when they're dancing in the streets. These carnival souvenirs were cheap looking, and when you picked up a handful of the colorful strung beads, most of them fell apart in your hand.

Drew, as usual, proved to be correct. Brazilian Exports, Ltd. solely existed as a front to launder criminally obtained money.

"Agent Lawrence nailed it," I reminded everyone. "This is a ghost company."

Soon, we located the central office. It proved easy to find, as all the other offices were empty. Nico found a wall safe behind a cheesy seascape. Russell used Hakim's miniature ultrasound device and his numerical engineer's mind to crack the combination and open the ancient, rusty iron safe in under ten minutes. Inside the antique vault, we discovered clue number three.

The clue turned out to be a huge stack of phone records with a lot of recent calls made to a satellite phone on Easter Island, lying on top of a pile of old-fashioned ledger books.

"Easter Island," Anya uttered, surprised. Then after thinking about it for a moment, she added, "Makes perfect sense. It's an extremely remote place."

"Yes," Chen-Jun eagerly agreed, "the perfect location to hide kidnap victims."

"Also apropos from an archaeological perspective," Russell added, nodding his head.

"Oh yeah," I said. "Especially since Dad and his team had a recent dig there—four or five months ago, I think."

"Ah yes, the remote island in the Pacific known for its mysterious statues," Hakim said, igniting a barrage of nervous chatter.

"Yes, yes," Nico said, "the island with the little statues."

"Not so *little*," Drew added. "Some of the statues are thirty-two feet tall and weigh eighty-two tons. Plus they were moved up onto a platform and into a row as much as twelve miles from where they'd been built. And all this in a time before the wheel had even been invented yet."

"And," Britton tossed in, "metal tools had not been invented yet either."

"Nothing like it in Malibu or anywhere down the Pacific Coast Highway," Jack threw in.

"We have many ancient, mysterious statues in Greece," Evangalia said, more stating fact than bragging.

"I'm glad this place has wireless," I heard Anya say, looking down at her iPad. "Give me a few minutes, and I'll have our transportation to Easter Island booked."

Soon, Team Eclipse was booked on a two-leg airline itinerary over the Internet that the FBI was no doubt monitoring. Which I had to admit, in this case I was glad about.

Chapter 18

Upon landing in Sao Paulo, Brazil, our second leg was on a chartered flight to Arturo Merino Benitez, a little outpost island in the eastern Pacific that had a boat waiting to take us over to Easter Island. Our chartered flight to this outpost was a bright yellow seaplane that seated twelve passengers and two pilots. It had been tricked out to fly long-distance over one of the largest expanses of open ocean in the world.

"Ethan, come in, Ethan, this is Anya, over."

I looked up and turned to her in the seat next to me. "Yes, Anya?" I asked. "Sorry, did you just say something?"

"Si," she said. "I asked if you have ever been to Easter Island before."

"No," I answered, "not yet, you?"

"Si, once," Anya informed me, "on a family trip to view the statues as tourists."

"Well, then good luck shines upon us," I said. "You know the place."

"By the way, knock it off, Ethan," she said.

"Knock what off?" I asked.

"This, this," she said, sweeping her long, beautiful fingers at me, "this pretense."

"Sorry, I'm still not following you."

"You know what I am talking about."

"You don't mean Evangalia?" I asked, finally catching on.

"Si, of course I mean Evangalia!" She rolled her eyes. "Who do you think I mean? Paris Hilton?"

I turned to her. "Anya, it's almost a thousand miles to Easter Island and a perfect time to grab some sleep." I paused. "To rescue my dad and his faithful team, we *all* need to get some sleep."

I closed my eyes to clearly signal the end of where this conversation seemed to be heading. *Now is not the time for this*, I told myself. *Even Anya can't argue with that.*

Soon I heard faint snoring sounds coming from the team, so I let go and caught some Zs.

Chapter 19

A brilliant sunrise woke me up, so I rolled over to get the sun out of my eyes and went back to sleep. When I woke, according to my watch, I had slept for another four hours. I couldn't go back to sleep, so I just sat there thinking how much I wanted to rescue my dad and his team from certain death. I started, well, positively meditating on this objective. Several hours later, after flying over a tremendous expanse of open ocean, we were landing in the Pacific and gliding up to a dock at the outpost to Easter Island.

"I'm glad you joined our team," I told Britton, leaping off the seaplane and jumping into a nearby boat that we'd hired to take us over to Easter Island.

"Me too, mate," Britton agreed. "Me too."

Abruptly, he leaned in further. "What's up with you and Anya?" he whispered. "If looks could kill, my friend, you'd be dead and buried."

"Yeah," I said, sighing. "Nico noticed that too."

"News flash!" Britton exclaimed. "We all have." He leaned in a bit closer. "Seriously, mate, what's the story with you two?"

"Well," I began, "we've been Skype-dating at least twice a week for almost a year now."

"But now you're in love with Evangalia," Britton said.

"Yes," I admitted. "Actually, she was my girlfriend before Anya."

"Yowser," Britton said, just before the open boat revved up and roared off. "A soap opera."

"Yeah," I said, "it's called, *As Your Stomach Turns*."

Immediately, as if to prove the stomach-turning point, the boat's twin engines clamored to life and started violently bouncing us up and down in our seats, hydroplaning over choppy waters that sloshed over the side of the craft and soaked us to the bone. The chaotic profusion of noise from the screaming roar of the engines made all conversation cease immediately. Despite the raucous ride over to Easter Island, I felt thankful for this.

At the dock, a van idled, waiting for us. James stared smugly at me from behind the wheel. On the road, I asked Lawrence for a briefing. He informed me that at this time there wasn't any confirmation that my dad and his team were still on the island. However, he did say that he had arranged for a temporary FBI headquarters camp for us to regroup and go over our next move.

"Why the camp?" I insisted. "If they're here on the island, we're just wasting time!"

"Every soldier knows that the formidable advantage in an attack is always surprise," Lawrence said. "It just so happens, Ethan, that in less than three hours there is going to be a total eclipse of the sun, and with it, as I'm sure you know, comes total darkness. We believe that your father and his team are being held in the underground bunker that Dr. Sparks excavated recently. It's on the other side of the island, and obviously it will be a much safer maneuver under the cover of darkness."

"Good idea," I said. "Definitely sounds like a plan to me."

Chapter 20

The ad hoc FBI camp had been slapped up on one of the remotest beaches on earth. Easter Island is located in the southeastern Pacific, at the southeastern most point of the Polynesian Triangle. It is famous for its prehistoric row of statues, called *Moai*. A relentless wind blew across ancient volcanic rock stripping the barren, mostly treeless land of its moisture and topsoil. There was a haunting beauty in this bleak and lonely landscape.

I looked around at the others investigating the perimeter of the camp. A tight, controlled space, lots of sand and brush mostly.

"Your father is close by," I heard Chen-Jun say. "I feel it."

"Me too," I said. "In fact, Lawrence and I think that they're being held in the bunker that Dad and his team recently excavated. A bunker that once housed the workers who constructed the statues during the time when they were building them."

I turned to him. "And after we rescue him, Dad's going to take us on a guided tour of these awesome statues." I paused.

"Boy," I chatted nervously, "I'm really looking forward to seeing them! It's still a mystery how prehistoric man constructed them without metal tools and then moved these tall soaring, massive tons of stone onto a platform to form a straight row during a time in ancient history where the wheel hadn't even been invented yet."

"How proud your father will be," Chen-Jun said, politely ignoring the fact that I had just been rambling.

Before I could respond to that, Lawrence called a meeting in the camp's command center.

"From Dr. Sparks's archaeological records," Lawrence said, starting his briefing, "we know that he and his team excavated a nearby lost underground colony. We believe that the doctor and his team are now being held in this colony."

"Makes sense to me that they have them stashed underground," I said. "It's a lot easier to contain them."

"It makes sense to us as well," Lawrence agreed. "We're heading out at O-Eleven-Hundred." He glanced at his watch. "That's two hours and six minutes from now. It's also when the total eclipse of the sun is forecasted. As you know, it's best to operate under the cover of darkness. I'd say that we're extremely fortunate that we happen to be here during such a rare event."

"This is a very, very good sign!" Evangalia said, pointing up to the heavens.

We all agreed, either verbalizing it or nodding.

"Okay," Lawrence said. "Now may I suggest grabbing something to eat? There's some breakfast in the mess tent."

"Hey," I managed to say, shoving down a sudden extremely bad gut feeling, "shouldn't we synchronize our watches?"

Chapter 21

The total eclipse of the sun turned out to be awesome! Pure, unfiltered darkness wrapped us in a safe cocoon of stealth and the concealment of one's intentions. For a spy, it doesn't get any better than this. I must admit, I felt an adrenalin-fueled exhilaration. This headiness led to a powerful hope that within the hour we would be rescuing my dad and his team.

Team Eclipse and the two FBI agents marched along a dirt road to the location of the underground colony. Special Agent Lawrence took the lead; Agent James contained the rear. I forced my way in as second in line.

Along the way, our infrared night goggles allowed us to see green-tinted dead-looking brown brush with mossy grass patches. There were rocks here and there with green leafy plants growing out of it. Also, I noticed entire ecosystems had formed inside the clusters of little rocks where rainwater had collected.

"The collection of water contained within these sporadic clusters of rock is what makes them grow," I suddenly heard Drew say behind me. "The only other fresh water on this island collects in the craters of the extinct volcanoes around here."

"Thanks," I said, walking down the ancient dirt road.

"The island is fairly hilly," Drew added.

"More like mountains," I said to him. "The hills are almost mountains."

"It's all relative in perception," Drew said, carrying the conversation on. "You see mountains, I see hills." He stopped. "Simply two different perspectives. Wouldn't you agree?"

I turned to my oldest friend in the world and said, "Let me guess. Scientifically, you are correct. These are hills, not mountains—not technically. Right?"

He nodded.

"This is a classic case of perception," we suddenly heard Chen-Jun say next to us. "E-than," he continued, "sees mountains, and I, just like you, know them to actually be hills."

"Quite right, perception is indeed the key here," Russell popped in, stating the obvious in that British way of agreeing with something that someone just said.

"I see them as mountains too," Nico slid in, "little mountains."

"Or very *big* hills," Britton Frisbeed in.

"*Enormous* hills," Jack agreed.

I stopped walking, then turned to face them.

"Okay, guys," I said. "I admit it. I embellish life a bit."

"As do we all, Sparks," Russell slipped in. "As do we all," he repeated more like a thought that he realized out loud.

"Still an odd landscape," Drew said to change the subject. "Wouldn't you agree?"

"Yes," I answered. "Yes, I would, especially the odd, stand-alone palm tree here and there."

"Hey," Hakim added out of the blue. "Did you know that there is an ancient road just above us?" He pointed up into the darkness. "The road is called Road Moai. It is a dirt road, very similar to the one we are on now, only Road Moai is the road where the ancient ones moved the extremely heavy stone statues."

"Along Road Moai there are also some statues that never made it to the platform to be lined up with the others," Anya added.

'Wow," I said.

"Cool!" Jack proclaimed. "I tell you, these statues are so cool."

"Yes," Evangalia agreed. "And to celebrate our victorious rescue of Ethan's father and his team, we should ask Dr. Sparks to take us on a tour of the famous statues."

I took in a deep, cleansing breath. "Yes, that is exactly how this mission will celebrate its victory," I said, keeping to myself that I had already thought of this.

"Hear, hear!" extolled Russell.

Oh yeah, I thought to myself. *We're amped!*

"All of you," James commanded, "back in line—now!"

Chapter 22

The secret underground colony had a hidden entrance that took a while for us to find.

"Here it is," Hakim finally said, using his new miniature Hollow Underground X-Ray Detector.

"Bingo," Britton said, excitedly scooping away the thick moss patches put there to effectively camouflage the wooden hatch. "Good thing we have Hakim's detector, or we would have walked straight past it."

I opened the wood hatch and saw a set of stone steps that disappeared into darkness. Hakim had this awesome miniature drone that looked like a mosquito. It even buzzed like one and had tiny, beady, red eyes that were actually a video camera. He released it down into the underground colony, and monitoring its video feedback on his phone, we saw that there weren't any guards—just a closed door. The drone couldn't even slip under its threshold because it didn't have one.

Lawrence insisted on being the first to walk down into the colony. As he walked down the creepy steps, I poked my head into the entrance hole, and my high-powered night goggles revealed that he had three more steps to go until he arrived onto a large landing that led into a wide hallway.

At the landing, Lawrence flicked on his penlight and gave us the thumbs-up, all-clear sign. I supervised the other team members as they ducked under the entrance hatch and descended the steps one by one to join Lawrence.

When it was Evangalia's turn, I tried to help her. Boy, did this make her mad. In fact, she swatted me Big Time on my head.

Rubbing the crown of my head, I walked down the steps, followed by James, our rear containment. The stone steps were ancient looking, even though the parts where they'd crumbled over the centuries had recently been repaired. The smell of pine cleaner cheered me with the hope that soon our rescue mission would be a success. My dad's ancient artifact cleaner of choice was pine-scented.

Suddenly, out of the corner of my eye, Agent Lawrence signaled for his partner to quickly join him at the front of the group. James immediately became a hulking human blockade that prevented us from proceeding down the hallway. With the perimeter secure and us contained within it, Lawrence took out his holstered firearm. The specially trained federal agent pointed his service revolver in a continuous left-to-right sway, then he unsealed the door that the mosquito drone couldn't penetrate.

When he returned, the expression on his face told me right away that Dad and his team were not there. I sighed Big Time, feeling the searing disappointment piercing my heart and stabbing my brain with abject disappointment.

"Let me check the place out!" I demanded. "If they were ever here, Dad would have left me a clue!"

Lawrence signaled to James to let me pass him, and then, escorted by the special agent in charge, I made my way past open storerooms with organized shelves of labeled containers, turned a corner, and walked into the main area of the ancient underground colony.

Chapter 23

As I followed Lawrence into the main area of the colony, I smelled feet. A good sign, because I have to admit it, Dad's feet definitely do not smell like roses when he's out in the field.

I thoroughly searched the room, scrutinizing it for any visual evidence that my father and his team had recently been there. I knew that they'd worked there three months ago and saw definitive evidence of this. The debris of the excavation had been sifted through, organized, bagged, and catalogued. Then they'd been stored on the shelves in those marked containers in the storerooms I'd just passed. A strong gut feeling told me to focus, channel even, on my dad's archaeological achievements in this room. It would be a viable, tangible way to stay connected to him.

So I made a conscious point of noting that the enormous, cavernous room had been newly restored. The bunker's once-deteriorated stone walls had been patched and reinforced with the same indigenous materials found on the island that the ancient

Polynesians had used when they first constructed it. The fact that the patch jobs were barely discernible proved to be a signature of my dad's team.

My father is renowned for being a perfectionist when it comes to his archaeological restorations. And he insisted that the carpenters on his team do a perfect job, often micromanaging them.

This bunker became one of my dad's projects because he believed that this colony once housed the ancient Polynesians while they were building the stone statues. At the time, they built one thousand massive stone figures that they believed were infused with the spirits of their ancestors. They even had eyes and facial features.

One of my dad's favorite statues had a red hat. But my father also *loved* PB&J sandwiches on rye bread with their crusts cut off and then sliced into four equal sections. Mom always packed a bunch of them in Dad's field pack. I found one of these sandwiches; it was still relatively fresh from its special airtight plastic wrap, hidden under one of the flimsy mattresses that belonged to a cot up against the rear wall.

"Dad and his team were definitely here," I said, holding up the section of sandwich he had left me as a visual clue. "That means that they've been moved *again*."

"Yes," Agent Lawrence agreed. "However, the trail has unfortunately gone cold. At this point, we have no idea what their twenty is."

"Their twenty," I repeated. "That's cop talk for their location, right?"

Agent Lawrence nodded.

"Well," I informed him, "we do have a clue what their *twenty* is." I flipped the section of sandwich over and showed him that a scrap of paper had been deliberately smooshed into its backside. On that scrap of paper, definitely scrawled by my dad in his familiar handwriting, turned out to be the word *hills*.

Drew, as always, is correct, I thought, sighing in total relief that the trail had not gone cold. *We were indeed surrounded by hills, not mountains.*

I turned to the FBI agent in charge. "Seems it's off to the hills we go!"

Chapter 24

It took us almost two hours to climb up into the hills. We immediately formed a linear search line and started combing the perimeter for any telltale signs that people either were presently in the area or at least had recently been there. I led this search, as it had been well established that Dad seemed to be leaving these visual clues for *me* to find.

Finally, after possibly an hour, maybe more, I came upon the burnt-out remains of a campfire. Britton, right behind me, picked up a handful of ashes, brought them close to his nose, inhaled deeply, and then proclaimed, "This is a recent fire, mate." He took in another whiff of the ashes. "Oh, my educated guess, I'd say, is that this fire was smothered about two hours ago."

"How can you tell?" I asked.

"An aborigine I met in the bush taught me how to gauge how long a campfire's been extinguished," the Aussie explorer answered. "Shortly after a fire's been put out, the ashes start turning into soot. The older the soot gets, the less acrid it smells."

"Huh," I said, nodding. "Makes sense to me."

I turned to Lawrence. "Well, Special Agent in Charge," I told him, trying unsuccessfully not to be angry about it, "seems that we made an error in judgment by hanging out in camp waiting for the cover of darkness to begin our rescue mission." I paused and took in a deep breath in an attempt to regain some calm. "My guess, as soon as the kidnappers found out that we'd arrived, they moved them. Also, I further speculate that they took them up here to board them on a helicopter."

"Wouldn't we have heard a helicopter big enough to hold ten or so people take off?" James asked.

"Not if we were underground at the time," I turned to the big galoof and answered.

"Precisely," Russell agreed. "The whirlybird took off while we were in the abandoned colony looking for them."

"Apparently, E-than," Chen-Jun pointed out, "the kidnappers' escape from us must have been a well-orchestrated plan. It would not have mattered when we went to the underground colony to begin our search; the captors already had them up here waiting for us to go underground so they would not be heard taking off."

"So, mate, it's best to keep a clear head, eh?" the sage nineteen-year-old advised. "Take things as they come, as you Yanks say."

"Yeah," I said, barely holding onto my center. "Obviously I should accept the fact that the kidnappers are one step ahead of us and just focus on finding the visual clue that my father left me so we can take our search mission to yet *another location*."

Everyone nodded, in complete agreement.

I closed my eyes, took a deep, steadying breath, and fought the impulse to tear the nearby landscape apart to frantically find the physical clue that I knew my dad had left for me to tell us where they'd taken them next.

While the others broke into their appointed sections of the surrounding area, I started flipping over spewed volcanic rocks, scratching through piles of dried brown brush, and kicking patches of mossy moisture-starved dirt that exploded in my face.

In time, my frustration escalated even more, forcing me to start furiously spinning around and around, deliberately trying to make myself dizzy so the anger would go away. I fell to the ground—and when my vision cleared, I noticed that someone had carved an arrow up the bark of a lonely stand-alone palm tree that pointed up to its fronds. I looked up and saw that that someone had also thrown a little bottle into the hollow of one of those palm fronds.

I climbed the tree, reached into the hollow, and removed a small bottle of seasick pills. Just like the ones my mom packed for Dad whenever he went on a dig where he had to travel by water.

Message: *We are not aboard a ship. We have been flown to the next place.* A confirmation of something we already suspected.

However, also in that hollow, hidden behind the pills, another clue that my father had left me suddenly peeked out at me. It surprised me to see the little, green-spotted rubber turtle that Dad had bought for me on our family trip to the Galapagos Islands when I was nine years old. For years, I'd taken baths with that little turtle, and then one day, I just lost it. Or so I had thought.

I had always wondered where that little, green turtle had gone. Now I knew; dear old Dad carried it with him on his archaeological digs as a good-luck charm.

We're like that, the Sparks. All of us, we each carry a good-luck charm. Mine is the compass Grandpa gave me when I turned twelve.

Mom calls it our connective idiosyncrasy. And she ought to know; she's the one who started it. Her charm is a locket with both of her sons' newborn pictures. I look like an ape; it's something Carter razzes me about.

Swinging from a tree branch, I held up the little, rubber turtle. "See this?" I announced. "I started to take baths with this turtle when we got back from our family vacation in the Galapagos Islands just after my ninth birthday." I paused. "This tells me that their new twenty is on one of the Galapagos Islands."

Chapter 25

Looking out my round window as the huge military helicopter flew to the Galapagos Islands, I had a strong gut feeling that Dad and his team would definitely be there when we arrived. To make sure that I had enough energy to rescue them, I closed my eyes and took a power nap.

"Only fifty-three minutes of flight time remaining until we approach the Galapagos Islands," our CIA pilot announced, waking me up.

"We caught a break," Lawrence said, sitting next to me. "According to a recent flyover, a massive underground heat signature leads us to believe that your dad's twenty is Wolf Island."

"Huh," I muttered, "another underground facility."

"Wolf Island," Drew said, across the aisle. "That's the remotest island there is in the Galapagos chain."

"I've been there," Anya interjected. "It's almost prehistoric.

Little has changed on that island since the volcanoes erupted and formed it."

"I'm guessin' we won't find any modern conveniences there," Britton tossed in.

"I have always wanted to visit the Galapagos Islands," Russell said. "I believe there are eight main islands, if I'm correct."

"You are most correct," Chen-Jun said, "there are indeed *eight* main islands, and they all straddle the equator. To be specific, they are 605 miles off the eastern Pacific coast of Ecuador."

"The equator!" Nico exclaimed. "Ecuador!" He turned to Evangalia. "We are *very* far away from home!"

"Always an adventure with Ethan," Evangalia said, giving me a wink.

"I have this feeling that my Hollow Underground Detector will come in handy on Wolf Island," Hakim said.

I turned to Agents Lawrence and James. "I see that the CIA is involved in this now."

"Yes," Lawrence confirmed. "The CIA is now involved in this joint operation because of Murphy. We take care of our own, even the one who retired to become your father's bodyguard."

"Huh," I said, "our own." *Seems our FBI friends are really CIA.*

Chapter 26

The enormous helicopter propelled by its three sets of whirling blades landed on one of the few level and clear patches on Wolf Island. One by one, we jumped out onto a huge rock ledge.

Geographically speaking, I could easily get distracted looking at the scenery. I shoved my love of photography and archaeology deep into my cargo pants pocket to try to remain focused on our mission. Still this place turned out to be totally awesome. Anya didn't exaggerate in the least; it looked almost prehistoric around there. Obviously, little had changed since all the volcanoes erupted and formed this fascinating place.

Wolf Island, named after the German geologist, Theodor Wolf, had been formed by tons of spewed-out volcanic rocks that landed everywhere centuries ago. And walking over these rocks, we headed to an area with a tent covering a small table with a map spread out on it. Once assembled, Lawrence started the briefing.

"Our Intel, which we believe to be reliable, tells us that Dr. Sparks and his team are currently being held at this location," Lawrence began, pointing to an area on the map close to the shoreline. "It is also believed from surveillance imaging that this location is a manmade underground cave."

We all looked at one another, as if doing so made this information less surprising.

"As you can see," Lawrence continued, "this cave dwelling is about a quarter of a mile from here—at a distance from the shoreline so as to utilize the Pacific as a filtered water source but not close enough to risk flooding even at high tide." He paused, allowing time for his Intel to be understood. "Obviously, a dwelling such as this must have cost millions. However, at this time, our forensic money trail has yielded absolutely nothing as to the identity of the owner of such a fantastic hideout, or home, or whatever the cave was constructed as."

"Do we at least know the size of this manmade underground cave?" I asked.

"Yes," Lawrence answered, "from the thermal heat-sensing perimeter scan that we performed aerially, it is estimated that the dwelling is between three or four thousand square feet."

"Wow!" I exclaimed. "My guess, it's a residence."

"Yeah," Britton tossed in, "and no doubt it has a Tuscany-style kitchen."

"Maybe even an indoor swimming pool," Nico added.

"Yes," Russell interjected with a slight admonishing tone, "however, we seem to be digressing."

"Yes," Lawrence agreed. "So let's stay on task, shall we?"

Everybody nodded.

"Good," the agent in charge said. "Now let's head out—the usual formation, a single line following me, with Agent James holding up the rear. Is this understood?"

Another mutual confirmation nod from Team Eclipse told the agent in charge that we understood his direct order. We started moving, but this time I squeezed my way in front of Agent James instead of following his partner. That way, Hakim could be at the front of the line and use his Hollow Underground Detector to locate the cave's front door. Hakim's device looked like a metal detector, except instead of just detecting metal, it also detected hollow underground space.

James tapped me on the shoulder just before the line started moving toward the shoreline. "So, Sparks, did you make up those stories in *The Young Explorer* magazine? Or are they true?"

"Both," I answered. "All of my articles are largely based on the truth."

"But embellished?" James pushed.

"You already know this," I baited him, on a fishing expedition, "because you read about it in my internal file, right?"

"Who told you that you have an Office file?" James said, answering my question. I also noted that he'd said "Office" file and not "Bureau" file. The CIA calls their headquarters the Office. The FBI refers to itself as the Bureau. I was right, they are really CIA.

I turned to the beefy Agent James and said, "You just did, when you told me that I have an Office file." I smirked. "Huh, seems that I have obviously generated enough possible recruitment interest, so much so to at least have an internal CIA file at fourteen."

"Who said that it's a CIA file?" James doth protested too much.

"Again," I informed him, "you just did."

"No, I didn't," he protested.

"Yes, you did," I told him. "You said that I had an *Office* file. I'm sure you know that the CIA calls its branches *Offices*, and the FBI calls itself the *Bureau*."

"Of course I know that," James said, sounding deflated. "I just didn't know that you knew that."

"Well, Agent James," I said, "there's probably a lot of things that you don't think I know that I know."

"This conversation is terminated," James insisted, barely managing not to show his flash of anger at my annoying teenage audacity.

I felt appreciative for the silence actually. I could hear the ocean waves just up ahead. Soon, we were trekking along the beach area, following Lawrence to the known location. Hakim trailed right behind him with his Hollow Underground Detector ready to identify the cave's entrance.

I saw hammerhead sharks circling close to shore.

I also saw a bird called a vampire finch—small birds with super-sharp beaks that drink the blood of the blue-footed boobies. To my surprise, the boobies just sat on a bunch of rocks jutting out into the Pacific and let them do it. Above us, swallow-tailed gulls circled. I got the impression they were sizing us up as a possible food source.

At the end of a cove, we hung a left and started trekking toward the basalts just above us. Basalts are what they call the terrain around here; basically, it's two layers of volcanic-spewed rock, one on top of the other, and usually gray in color; but as the sun set casting an eerie light, the layers of rock appeared to be rust-red.

The top layer of the basalt's terrain is a caldera, the remains of a mountainous volcano that once exploded like, I don't know, maybe even worse than a nuclear blast.

The caldera had eroded over the centuries. It made the top layer of rock unstable and very uneven, with lots of pitfalls and a definite watch-where-you-walk type of terrain.

Then I spotted it, another of Dad's visual clues, a shred of his favorite yellow work shirt. The one with the two black outlined front pockets. Dad had tucked it into the reddish-gray rock ledge so I would see it.

"Another clue!" I exclaimed. "The cave is down here." I pointed. "Right where I'm standing."

"Yes," Hakim confirmed, "and my detector is picking up a huge piece of metal. It is my educated guess that we have found the entrance to the cave."

Working together as a team, we moved what turned out to be a light piece of fake rock ledge. Underneath, we saw a cast-iron submarine-hatch-like door, the kind you open by turning an enormous wheel.

We opened the door to the cave and then looked down and saw a set of stone steps. Hakim released his mosquito drone, and one by one, led by me, we walked down the steps following the miniature drone on camera. I felt wicked cold air that made me shiver like someone dead passed through me from the grave.

At the bottom, a well-lit, spacious foyer opened wide into a hallway that looked like an art gallery. In ornate, gilded frames there were rows of paintings hanging on both sides of the walls. These oil paintings and watercolors all appeared worthy enough to be on display in a museum. *And yet*, I realized, *they're hanging in the entrance to a cave.*

I also noticed that security cameras followed us with tiny, red, blinking lights. Still, I defiantly led the team down the hall until we came to a set of double doors.

I opened the door, and much to my surprise, there stood Spiros Stepanopolis—the middle-aged, pint-sized Greek billionaire with a prosthetic right leg and a vicious little spider monkey on his shoulder named Pou-Pou. Two years ago, Nico, Evangalia, and I had outwitted him in Greece. He should have been rotting away in prison until he turned eighty or ninety for stealing priceless Greek artifacts, but somehow he got out, probably bribed his way to freedom. Money can buy a lot of things.

But what really disturbed me was that behind Spiros stood Dad and his team, *and they each had bombs strapped to them.*

I glared at Spiros. He smiled and held up a little, solid-gold device, obviously the trigger to the bombs.

Boom, he mouthed, smirking at me. Then that annoying, demented little monkey of his threw his hands up in the air to mimic an explosion!

I wanted to smack the hubris off both of their faces.

Chapter 27

"Hi, Dad," I said, staring at the digital bomb strapped to his favorite yellow shirt, the one that now had a tear in its sleeve so that he could leave me a shred of it tucked into the caldera's rock as a visual clue.

"Hello, son," Dad said, noticeably sighing. "See you found all my clues and figured out their messages." He smiled proudly. "I knew you would."

"Loud and clear," I told him.

Then I looked at Murphy, my dad's bodyguard, a former CIA op, and my friend. Murphy's enormous head nodded only once, but that said it all.

"A true father-and-son reunion," Chen-Jun said.

"Finally!" Anya noted.

"How nice," Spiros said, sarcastically.

"Oh, I don't agree," Russell said, directly challenging Spiros's statement. "Admittedly, it would indeed be a much happier reunion if the hostages did not have bombs strapped to them with preignition activation already in place."

"You mean the little, blinking, red lights," Nico said, pointing.

"Perhaps we could all just be civil," Spiros said. "Have tea maybe, or a Yoo-hoo?"

"I'll take a little Yoo-hoo," Jack said. He turned to me and mouthed, *He's crazy.*

"I'll take a Yoo-hoo too," Britton said, gesturing the crazy sign.

"As will I," Chen-Jun said.

"Also me, please as well," Hakim added.

"I don't know what a Yoo-hoo is," Nico said, throwing his hand down in resignation, "but I guess I'll take one too."

"It's a chocolate soda drink," Drew said, "usually comes in small bottles. I'll take one too, I guess."

"Okay," I said to the crazy Greek billionaire. "That will be six Yoo-hoos so far, including mine."

I turned to the CIA partners, Lawrence and James, and the girls. "Want a Yoo-hoo?" I asked them.

The four of them nodded their heads.

I turned back to Spiros. "So that's twelve Yoo-hoos for all the new guests. What about the old ones? You know," I said to him, "the doctor and his team."

"They love Yoo-hoo as well," Spiros said, with a smug upturn of his chin. "So I will order Yoo-hoos for all my *guests*, old and new. And just to your left," he informed us, pointing, "we have a grand salon where we can all have a comfy chat."

"Did you ask them?" I said, pointing to my dad and his team.

"Did you ask them if having a preignited digital bomb strapped to their chests felt *comfy* to them?"

"Do you mean physically or emotionally?" Spiros asked.

"Both," I answered.

"Are you kidding?" Spiros said, sounding very serious. "They've all been living like kings and queens, eating me out of cave and home."

He laughed.

"They have very decent appetites for supposed kidnap victims is all I am saying," Spiros explained. "And they sleep in very suitable quarters, each in their own room with an en-suite bath," Spiros added, like they really were guests in his home.

"Let me guess," I said. "You tried to get cable out here but couldn't. Anyway, thanks for taking such good care of them. However," I added, quite seriously, "*now the visit is over.*" I stopped, eyed him but good. "We all want to leave now."

"Unfortunately, I cannot allow this," Spiros said, shrugging.

"Now, please, come in, everybody," he insisted, walking through a massive arch into an enormous room. "Let us chat a bit."

"A quirky little guy," Britton whispered to me as we were making our way from the big front hall into the grand salon, as Spiros had called it.

"Quirky," I repeated, turning to Britton. "I call it crazy."

"Crazy is so subjective, dude," Jack chimed in on his way past.

Wow, I thought, *no doubt this little get-together will prove nasty. Spiros is not getting the Elgin Marbles, and he knows it.*

My guess, Spiros wants payback for us thwarting him in Greece when we got our revenge with Poseidon's trident.

Chapter 28

"Spiros may be quirky," I whispered, sitting next to Britton, "but he's also very dangerous."

"I know," the Aussie surprised me by saying. "I read your Greece article in *The Explorer*. In fact, mate, I've read all five of your articles." He looked up. "Good stuff. I truly enjoyed reading them. You write them so visually; it's like you take us with you on the adventure."

"Thanks," I said, meaning it.

"Quite, quite adventurous," Britton added, fishing.

"They're *mostly* true," I told him. "I just add a little *attention-grabbing* insurance when necessary. You know, a few embellishments, shall we say, to keep the article interesting."

"And also to portray yourself as a big, strong hero," Anya suddenly said, brushing past me on her way to the couches and chairs.

"Literary license," I said, smirking at her.

"Yeah, yeah," Anya said, with a dismissive wave, sitting as far away from me as she could get.

Soon, we were all seated—all twelve members of Team Eclipse, my dad, his eight-member archaeological team, and of course our "host" Spiros. Also present in the room, on red alert, stood Murphy, Dad's bodyguard. He was severely unshaven, roughed up even—so different from Dad and the rest of his team who were, well, lookin' pretty good.

We were seated comfortably in a cavernous stone room with very comfy overstuffed couches and chairs, indirect lighting from strategically placed lamps, and one entire wall that was a huge, seamless glass aquarium teaming with at least a hundred vibrant and colorful east Pacific fish.

The décor in the room glowed in *earth tones,* as my mom calls them. *Honestly, this living room should be named the grand salon.* Britton may have been joking, but the cave probably did have a Tuscany-style kitchen. This place cost some serious coin.

All the money it took to build this place, I realized. *Why would Spiros risk losing all this by kidnapping my dad and his team and calling attention to its location? I've gotta admit, it's the perfect lair for a fugitive that should still be in prison for artifact theft.*

I looked over at our host. Tiny Spiros sat perched in a chair on stilts that had obviously been designed to make him appear taller. So far, the five-foot billionaire held all the cards in this twisted game of revenge.

Oh yeah, I thought, *Spiros is definitely holding the cards—a full house, in fact. But a royal flush will beat a full house. And together, Team Eclipse will flush Spiros and his goons right down the toilet.*

We also have Murphy, the ex-CIA operative, and a really tough guy, I reminded myself. *He* always *pulls through. He* always *has a plan.*

I glanced over at him. *What's the plan?* I mouthed to him.

Don't have one yet, he mouthed back.

Time to devise one, my lips silently said to him.

Murphy nodded.

"Well," Spiros asked, cutting through the awkward silence, "what shall we chat about?"

"How about the reason that we're here," I suggested, holding a Yoo-hoo in my hand and barely remembering being served it by a waiter.

"Why, to see my new, even more extensive artifact collection," he said, casually crossing his prosthetic leg, causing it to click.

"Oh, I see," I said, nodding, "you're still mad that we took your old collection away from you."

"Yes," he admitted. "I am."

"So this is revenge then, isn't it?" I asked.

"Absolutely!" he exclaimed, throwing both hands up in the air. "This is most certainly *revenge!*"

"As the ancient Chinese wisdom says," Chen-Jun warned, "when one sets out to seek revenge, one should dig two graves."

"Oh," Spiros said, with his index finger up and a twisted, menacing grin, "but graves will not be necessary in this case, you see. For you will all be blown into little *itty-bitty* bits." He paused. "Then I will simply have my staff scoop up the mess you've made and feed you to the sharks that live in the backyard." He paused, deliberately raising his perfectly manicured eyebrows into crossed swords and bestowed upon us the most I'm-so-much-more-clever-than-you smirk he could muster. "Perhaps," he continued, "you noticed all the hungry hammerhead sharks circling the island on your way here?"

He waited for an answer, but we all just ignored him.

"Well," he said, sounding indignant at our rudeness, "I'm sure you did. Every morning, Theo, my chef, feeds them the leftovers. However, very soon, the sharks will get a real treat—pieces of your tasty carcass," he added, staring directly at me.

Suddenly, his twisted smile took on a ridiculously crazy smirk of satisfaction. "You see," he said, as if he thoroughly enjoyed sharing this bit of info, "I had my bomb techs rig the explosive devices to basically only sever the top of your bodies from the bottom so that the sharks will get a substantial breakfast."

I just looked at Spiros, gave him a long fart-sounding raspberry, and said, "I'm not afraid of you."

Chapter 29

Apparently, Spiros's menacing threat resulted in a delayed reaction on my part, especially when the demented billionaire started laughing at my classically trained raspberry. I found myself leaping from my seat and wrapping my arms around Spiros's neck with this, well, involuntary need to choke him to death. Somehow, reason came to me just in the nick of time, and I stopped trying to kill him. Still, my act of aggression toward Spiros caused his vicious little monkey, Pou-Pou, to bare his teeth at me Big Time just before sinking his teeth into my hand.

"No, Pou-Pou," Spiros insisted, rubbing his throat. "Sit!" The pint-sized weirdo then started petting his vicious little monkey on his chin, just under his white-bearded mouth. "Ethan," he said to me, "I would advise you to sit as well." He paused. "You remember, dear boy, that on our—what shall we call it—*altercation* several years ago in Greece, my precious little Pou-Pou did not like you very much."

"Well," I said, going back to my seat and taking a clean white handkerchief from Russell to bind my wound, "since we're going down memory lane here, let me say, our *altercation*, as you call it, turned out to be Mandras, your little brother, Nico, Evangalia, and I stopping you from adding Poseidon's trident to your beloved but *stolen* antiquities collection."

"Yes." Spiros nodded. "Sadly, I do not have any of these pieces in my current collection."

"However," my father quickly interjected to stop me from angering Spiros even more, "your current artifact collection is quite impressive."

"Thank you," Spiros said, chewing on my dad's sedative. "I have a true respect for these records from our ancient past. This is why I am taking excellent care of them."

I looked at my father. "Well, Dad," I said, "Spiros may have stolen his current collection of archaeological artifacts, but at least he's preserving them as if they were in a museum."

"Yes," Evangalia kicked in, "but these precious artifacts are in a museum where only one man gets to see them."

"Not true," Spiros said, defensively. "My staff gets to see them, as well as my many, many trusted friends who come to visit, including, recently, your father and his team."

"Yeah," I said, "with bombs strapped to their chests."

"Now, now, Ethan," Spiros warned, wagging his finger at me. "Be nice, and I'll let you and your little entourage see my recent collection as well."

I suddenly heard my dad loudly clear his throat, his way of insisting that I play along instead of aggravating our nemesis.

"All right," I agreed, playing along. "I'm sure my team and I can't wait to see your little collection."

"Not so little," Dad said, clearly to inform us.

Spiros's eyebrows climbed his forehead sarcastically as he winked at me. "By the way, Ethan, the bombs are set to go off if anyone crosses the threshold to the cave. So, I would remember that if you plan on trying to escape in the middle of the night."

"Thank you," I said, winking back, "I will."

"Now," my father insisted, "your monkey bit my son on the hand—and he requires medical attention."

"Pou-Pou is up to date on all his shots," Spiros said. "He will be fine."

"Nonetheless," Dad managed, barely holding onto his patience, "I insist that my son see a doctor very soon."

"Oh! Yes! Yes!" Spiros exclaimed. "Demitri is a physician's assistant. He will dress Ethan's well-deserved wound and give him any shots that may be necessary." Then, yelling, we all heard Spiros call out, "Demitri! Demitri! We need you! And bring your medical bag!"

Chapter 30

We all had private rooms—the twelve of us and the ten kidnapped victims with initially activated bombs strapped to their chests. The residence also had a five-member staff—a chef, a server, a physician's assistant, and two goons. Basically, they were servants employed to attend to Spiros and his vicious little monkey's every need.

Wow, I realized, *this cave must be enormous. This place is definite proof of what evil billionaires can create.*

I finished the first shower in days, turned off the solid-gold faucets, then removed a fresh set of clothes from my backpack and dressed. When I walked into my room, Murphy was sitting on a chair waiting for me.

I put my finger to my mouth and gave him the *shoosh* sign. He nodded, and I punched the appropriate button on my watch and walked around the room sweeping it for bugs. The green, luminous scanner in the face of my watch dial told me that there was only one bug to deactivate. I made the appropriate sounds of getting into bed and going to sleep, silently counted to sixty; and then punching another button on my watch while pointing to the active bug, I jammed it from operating any further.

"Boy, you must have been an awesome spook when you were a field op in the CIA," I said, sitting across from him. "I never heard you come in."

"Took you long enough," Murphy said.

"Well, I haven't taken a shower in days," I reminded him.

"I'm not talking about the length of your shower," he said, shaking his head. "I meant for you to get here. We left you enough clues."

"Listen," I told him, "it's not easy when you're traveling in a pack of twelve."

"I guess." Murphy sighed, shrugging his shoulders.

"We should discuss our rescue plan quickly," I told him, "before they catch on that I just deactivated the bug in my room."

"Yeah," he agreed. "We should. Do you happen to have an extraction strategy in mind?"

"Not yet," I admitted. "I'm hoping that you already came up with one. I mean, you've had, what, three days to think about it while we were chasing visual clues around the globe to obtain your twenty."

"I guess that's true, and we'll just have to wait for the right opportunity to present itself to make our escape." He shrugged. "At least you have the advantage of knowing our *host* since you've already collared him once."

"Oh yeah," I said. "I think I know how Spiros thinks pretty

well. Still, the little billionaire and his twisted monkey are unpredictable."

"That's an understatement," Murphy said. "And obviously so are you—unpredictable, that is. You lost back there, Ethan, when you tried to choke Spiros. First rule of effective ops work: don't show your emotion."

"Duly noted," I said. "Now can we move on?"

"Yes," he deemed, "we can. Just don't let it happen again. Understood?"

I nodded. "Yes, I understand, and don't give me that cop face, please."

"Okay," he agreed, nodding back. "Now let's talk about the fact that your father and his team have bombs strapped to their chests and that Spiros has the detonator with him at all times."

"That's foremost on my mind," I assured him. "In fact, that plays heavily in the reason I don't have an escape plan yet." I paused. "The reason it has to be executed the first moment possible."

"So our plan," Murphy said, "is for you and me to be ready for the first possible chance to snatch the detonator from our host. It will just have to play out, basically be the most accessible opportunity at the time. I'm sure that Lawrence and James will immediately take our cue and jump on board with us without hesitation."

"Sounds like a plan to me," I said. "By the way, Murphy, they're CIA, aren't they—not FBI?"

Murphy's big bull neck nodded affirmatively. "They're the last two recruits I trained before leaving the agency. I guess you can say we bonded."

"They are loyal," I said.

"Loyal enough to allow you and your team to assist in this op," Murphy informed me. "Well, good night," he said, getting up. "I hear you have the first watch with Agent Lawrence. Of course you'll brief him on our conversation."

"Affirmative," I said, nodding.

Murphy left. I looked at my watch, reactivated the bug, and saw that I had four hours to grab some shut-eye before the first watch started at 2:00 a.m.

Chapter 31

The alarm on my watch beeped. *Time to get up*, I immediately registered, jumping out of bed. In less than five minutes, I joined my first watch partner, Agent Lawrence. As planned, we met in the broom closet off the kitchen. I had swept this closet earlier for bugs with my watch and did it again now for reconfirmation. Like before, the closet proved to be bug-free.

"Are Spiros and his goons asleep?" I asked Lawrence.

"Affirmative," he responded.

"Murphy and I had a chat," I told him. "Our exit strategy is still undefined at this time. The bombs strapped to their chests make this an ad hoc situation. Basically, our plan is to seize the first possible opportunity to gain possession of the detonator from Spiros."

"I imagine," the field op said, nodding, "that Murphy and you will be ones who instigate this."

"Yes," I said, "and once we do, I'm sure that you and James will back us up."

"Of course," Lawrence said. "In fact, I'm sure the entire ops team will immediately jump into action after your cue."

"Since we have this covered now," I said, "I have a personal question."

"Shoot."

"I know that I have a file at the Office," I began. "What's in it?"

"Well, let me first preface by saying that it's your creativity that first captured our attention. The name Ethan Sparks is well known back at the Office. Let's just say your accomplishments started adding up and became of interest to us," he informed me.

"Well, information is power, as they say," I joked.

"You may be joking," Lawrence said, "but it is. It's what gets you noticed. In your case, it's made you desirable for recruitment."

"I always thought I'd be a photojournalist," I told him. "But I have to admit it, becoming an operative is definitely appealing."

"The photojournalist slant would make a great cover," Lawrence said, "especially since you're so good at both."

"Careful, Agent Lawrence," I warned him, "my parents are always telling me I have a big ego. Keep talking, and it might become *enormous*."

Lawrence laughed. "Don't worry, Ethan. The Agency will help you keep your ego in check."

"Are you sure?" I asked him. "It's obvious to me that the Agency didn't keep Murphy's ego in check. His head is huge." I grinned. "And I'm talking both literally and figuratively."

"Huh, right you are," Lawrence said, smiling. "Good point."

He paused, and his beaver-like smile suddenly reverted to its serious expression. "You may or may not know this," he confided, "but Murphy is my mentor—that's why when he started talking highly of you, I listened."

"I'm glad you did," I said, not even pretending to be humble, "because my team and I are without a doubt an asset to this op."

"Yes," Lawrence said, his beaver smile returning. "I can see that."

Chapter 32

Wow, I reflected, once Lawrence and I had relinquished our post to Evangalia and Anya. *Are you kidding me? Obviously, Chen-Jun has a sense of humor. Why else would he schedule both my first and second girlfriends together as the next watch partners? You know that they're gonna talk about me.*

I had planned to be present at each and every shift change, but opted out of shift two since it turned out to be Evangalia and Anya's.

To stop thinking about this, I made my way to a dark corner in the kitchen and waited, soon zoning out, perhaps even nodding off a bit.

"I am supposed to meet you for shift three in the broom closet," Chen-Jun whispered in my ear, surprising me.

"Sorry," I whispered back. "I got sidetracked. Actually, I'm avoiding Anya and Evangalia. I'm sure you can understand why."

"I understand," Chen-Jun said, trying to hide his smile of amusement. "I'll let the girls know it's the end of their shift."

"Okay," I said, "I'll just hide here in the corner."

He nodded and walked into the broom closet. Moments later, the girls left without seeing me.

I joined Chen-Jun in the broom closet off the kitchen.

"You must be in much distraction. Even have a very, very big worry," Chen-Jun said, starting the conversation.

I nodded.

"No need to feel embarrassed," Chen-Jun said. "I understand what you are going through."

Then he looked me in the eye and added, "Well, perhaps not *fully* understand, as no one has ever kidnapped my father before."

He paused.

"Still," he continued, "I understand family, the love of family, both during the good times and the bad ones."

I looked at him. "Then you qualify to sympathize but not empathize," I said. My mother had explained this complex comparison to me just recently. I took in a deep breath. "I'm sorry, my friend. I'm losing it here. I tried to choke the little creep to death."

"I understand," Chen-Jun said, bowing his head. "I believe it is best for you not to be so emotional. It will help you to become stronger in spirit." Then he looked up and asked, "Do we have an escape strategy yet? Having one in mind I am sure will help you through this."

"Well, yes and no."

"May I inquire please? Is it more yes or more no?"

"I guess more yes," I said. "At this time, our plan is to seize the moment the second it becomes available."

"I would imagine," Chen-Jun said, "that obtaining the detonator from Spiros is our number-one priority."

"Definitely," I agreed. "In fact, my seizing the detonator will be the cue for us to begin our escape."

"This makes logical sense to me," Chen-Jun said. "We should not have too much difficulty after this, as there are so many of us and so few of them."

"You're right," I agreed. "But make sure you watch out for that vicious little monkey, Pou-Pou. He's a mean one."

"Good point," Chen-Jun said, nodding.

"Well, now that business is over," I said, "maybe you can tell me what you've been up to lately."

"I have just recently passed the test to go to college in my country," Chen-Jun said, proudly.

"Congratulations! Did you decide yet what you'll be studying?"

"Yes!" he answered, excitedly. "I have decided to become a scientists that specializes in de-extinction."

"De-extinction?" I asked. "What's that? Bringing things back to life?"

"Yes, precisely, and it is fascinating," Chen-Jun answered. "We can actually bring back extinct species, birds for instance, by using their DNA found in stuffed exhibits in a museum."

"Wow!" I exclaimed in awe. "That is fascinating!"

"Tell me, E-than," he asked, "have you decided what profession you will become?"

"I have," I answered. "I'm going to be a CIA agent pretending to be a photojournalist as my cover."

"Of course," Chen-Jun said, "it is very, very logical since you are already *so* good at both."

"I am," I agreed, trying to keep my ego out of it. Well, let's just say that I tried to be as humble as I could be, although I don't know why. When you're good at something, you should just acknowledge it and put it out there.

Chapter 33

Britton arrived to replace Chen-Jun for shift four.

"Hey, mate," Britton said. "Weren't you supposed to be the first shift? I'm number four, and you're still here."

"E-than has decided that he will join each shift," Chen-Jun said, waving good-bye.

"Ah, a bit of a control freak, eh," Britton said, achieving a bull's-eye in his metaphorical game of darts.

"Yes," I admitted. "I'm definitely a control freak." I looked at him. "And I come by it honestly. Both my parents are very accomplished and highly functioning control freaks."

"So you're sayin' you're genetically predisposed?" Britton said. I nodded.

"I understand, mate," Britton said. "I too have a bit of a need to control things as well. Get the trait from me parents as well."

"Well, I guess since you're the CEO of your own adventure company," I said, shrugging, "you do need to control things."

"Clever, mate," Britton said, nodding. "I too like a bit of rationalization now and then."

"Ha-ha," I said, smirking.

"I have to tell you," he said, taking on a sudden serious tone, "that I've noticed that if I allow fear to sneak up on me, I really get the urge to control—then my need to control totally controls me."

I looked at him. "Huh, you're sayin' that fear causes my need to control and totally take over."

"Just my observation," he said. "I have several observations and opinions, mate. Believe it or not, some of them even impress me."

"I'm guessin' it's more than *several*," I found myself saying. "In fact, I'd say there are quite a few."

The nineteen-year-old laughed. "That's brilliant, mate," he admitted, "and quite correct, I might add." He paused, giving me a sideways glance. "And since the cat's out of the bag, as you Yanks say, let me tell you my opinion on what fear stands for."

I nodded.

"F-e-a-r," he said, spelling it out, "is quite literal actually. It stands for *false evidence appearing real*."

"Did you make that up?" I asked him.

"Nah, heard it somewhere in my travels," he answered.

"Well, I like it," I told him. "And you're right, my need to control is definitely a rationalization to hide my fears."

"Speaking of rationalization," Britton asked, nodding his appreciation of our real moment, "do we have an escape plan yet?"

"We do," I told him. "Basically, Murphy and I will just seize the moment and grab the detonator out of Spiros's little hand the second the opportunity presents itself."

"Ah, carpe diem!" Britton exclaimed. "I like it! It's actually quite brilliant, mate! Perfectly simple, no fuss, a perfect strategy!"

"I have a good feeling about its success too," I said. "And I have to tell you, even though our plan is basically ad hoc, I still see it going down as a well-orchestrated maneuver because our team has so many skills that naturally work so well together."

"I have an opinion, well, more of a *suggestion*," Britton said.

"I would have been surprised if you didn't."

"Brilliant, mate," Britton said, smiling, "and yet your surprise appears more sarcastic than your tone implies."

I looked at him.

"You see, mate," Britton informed me, "it so happens that I can read eyebrows. And your eyebrows just pinched together like an old mum's look of disapproval; that tells me that you were being sarcastic. My guess, you weren't surprised at all that I had a suggestion to enhance our little escape plan."

"Well, I think there's humor in sarcasm," I said, deliberately stretching my eyebrows as far left and right as they would go.

"Yes, well let's not lose track of my suggestion," he said, dramatically squeezing his eyebrows together.

"No," I said, grinning. "So tell me, what is your suggestion?"

"I think Spiros has an enormous ego," he began, "and my suggestion is to play up to it. You know, mate, keep him on the rails."

"A very good idea," I agreed. "Spiros may be my pocket nemesis, but he has an enormous ego, and if he believes that we're at his mercy, it will feed his delusions."

"Precisely," he said, nodding. "The man does indeed hold onto his delusions; that's for sure."

"Oh yeah," I agreed, "Big Time. Besides, very little really operates on a true reality anyway. It's more just one's perception of reality."

"And when one's perception is driven by his delusions," Britton added, "then his actions become the manifestation of his thoughts."

"Oh yeah," I said, following his insight to its logical conclusion, "and that means his intention is an accelerant."

"Umm," Britton added, bobbing his head in total understanding, "an accelerant that makes his primary thought ultimately go boom."

"That's why I have to grab that solid-gold detonator out of Spiros's sweaty, little hand before he pushes the button to explode the bombs."

Chapter 34

Drew replaced Britton for shift number five.

Drew Tyler Macallister, my oldest friend in the world.

We met our first day at Montessori, and in no time we were on our first pretend spy op.

We went on many, many cool spy missions. Special ops like saving Bolivar or rescuing some Danish king from certain death. And sometimes we just shored up the perimeter, keeping it safe from enemy agents. Drew has a photographic memory. All he has to do is look at something or read it once, and he has total recall of it.

"Well, Ethan," Drew said, right out of the bullpen. "It seems to me that your obsessive need to control precluded your need to get some REM sleep."

"Yup," I said. "Actually, I couldn't totally let go and sleep even if I wanted to."

"Anxiety," Drew said. "I hope it's not a *bad* gut feeling?"

"Yes," I admitted to him. "I need to control the operation at this point because of my feelings of anxiety due to fear," I confided. "It's just like you said, only without the presence of a bad gut feeling."

He looked at me. "Wow. Well, I have to say, that's honest."

"Yeah," I said, nodding, "Britton helped me to see that my need for control is my way of dealing with the anxiety that's caused by my fear pattern."

"Um," he said, nodding back, "I do that too."

"Yes," I nodded, "I know. Seems we both do it as some form of rationalization."

"Well, you also come by it naturally," Drew pointed out. "Everyone in your family is super-talented at what they do. Heck, they're even a bit arrogant because of it."

"It's more my mom and Carter," I told him. "Not as much Dad and I."

Drew stopped. When he swept the mop of shaggy, brown hair out of his eyes, I saw those pupil twitches that he gets when he's deep in thought.

"You know, you're right," Drew said, sounding, well, surprised that he hadn't realized this himself.

"Well, don't be so surprised," I told him. "The older I get, the more I understand my family's dynamics."

"A family," Drew said, "that would go to the ends of the earth to ensure one another's well-being."

I turned to him. "Yeah, obvious, isn't it?"

"I know it's sappy," Drew said, shrugging his shoulders. "But love, that's what's important in a family. And your family really loves one another."

He stopped. "By the way, speaking of love," he said. "I'm dating Stephanie Macintire."

"No kidding," I said. "You've been predating each other since the eighth grade." I smiled. "Finally, it's official!"

"Speaking of official," Drew asked, "do we have an established escape plan?"

"Boy," I said, sighing, "it sure would be easier if we all could have a strategy meeting."

"Everyone's asked you that question already?"

"Yup."

"Mind going over it again then?"

"Nope," I said, shrugging. "Basically, it's carpe diem."

"Ah, seize the moment."

"You got it."

"Sounds like a plan to me." He paused. "By the way, I'm sure this won't surprise you, but I have a suggestion."

"I would have been shocked if you didn't," I told him. "Everyone else did too."

"Were they helpful?"

"Absolutely." I grinned. "And I know yours will be too."

"That's not sarcasm, is it?"

"No, I'm serious." I shrugged my shoulders. "You know that old saying. Everyone's got an opinion."

"Ethan," Drew said, "stop complaining."

"I'm not complaining," I insisted. "I'm expressing my thoughts."

"Good," Drew said, putting us back on track. "Now, my

suggestion is for me to divert Spiros so you can strike when he least expects it."

"Ah," I said, "it's our standard operating procedure. You divert the subject while I rip the rug out from under him. I'm guessing that you'd like me to give you our secret sign when to start this procedure."

"Affirmative," Drew said, his eyes slanting knowingly like he always does when we've developed a strategy. "Now can we talk a bit about my very first girlfriend, Stephanie?"

"Absolutely," I answered.

So we did.

Chapter 35

Suddenly the broom closet door creaked—it opened, and in sauntered Jack.

"Hey, dudes," Jack said, smiling. It was exactly that smug smile I remembered so well from our Mexican rain forest adventure.

"You're late," Drew said. "Shift five is on the schedule at 0:500." He pointed to his watch. "That was thirteen minutes ago."

"Sorry, man," Jack responded, shrugging. "I'm just not as anal as you."

I grinned, turned to my old friend and we fist-bumped. "See you, Drew, at 0:700 for breakfast, as scheduled."

When Drew left, I turned back to Jack. "Before you ask, we have an exit strategy. And yes, I'd like to hear your suggestions on how to grow it."

"Wow, *grow it*," Jack said, smirking at me, the puka shells on a leather strap around his neck glinting. He laughed. "You know, as opposed to *enhance it*, which is more Ethan-like."

"Don't laugh at me," I insisted.

"I'm not laughing *at* you," he said, shrugging. "I'm laughing *near* you."

"Jack," I said, "I thought we were past this; friends now even."

"Only on Facebook," he said.

"Anyway," I said, shrugging. "It's obvious that you still have a problem staying focused on the big picture. Our Anya rivalry still gets in the way, I see."

"Maybe," Jack admitted, "but it's obvious that you're still suffering from know-it-all syndrome."

"That's not a real thing."

"See."

"Back, Jack," I insisted, "to the exit strategy. Remember?"

"Still wearin' your bossy pants, huh," Jack said, with his smug smile and puka-shell glint.

"Still mad about Anya, I see," I countered.

"Not anymore," he said. "It's pretty obvious that you've moved on to Evangalia once again."

He paused, obviously realizing something important. "Whoa, dude, that means that Anya will soon need an old friend to comfort her from her loss of the old Ethan charm."

"I wish you luck, Jack," I said, realizing something myself. That it was true, I did want Evangalia back.

"Wow," Jack said. "You sounded, well, *sincere*."

"I am being sincere," I told him. "You think I have bossy pants—well, wait till you get to know Anya better and her bossy dress." I paused, gave him a grinning nod, then added, "That's why I sincerely wished you good luck."

He looked at me. His smug smile started to flicker on and off like it had a loose wire. "Dude," he said, "don't get existential on me."

"Okay, *dude*," I said, speaking his language. "Are we gonna grow our exit strategy or not?"

"Obviously not," Russell answered, abruptly walking in. "Shift six reporting to the broom closet on time as scheduled."

Chapter 36

"Well, Sparks," Russell said, when Jack had left, "seems that you're not everyone's cup of tea, as we Brits sometimes say."

"Jack's still mad that I got the girl after our rain forest adventure," I explained.

"Yes," Russell said, with his proper British pretense. "One doesn't have to be even slightly clever to see that."

I sighed, looking sarcastically at him. "Are you going to help grow our exit strategy or not?"

"Sorry, Sparks," the seventeen-year-old with a master's in engineering from Oxford said sincerely. "Of course—and we only have, what?" He looked down at his watch. "Less than twenty minutes until the next shift."

"Thanks." I nodded. "Especially since our current exit strategy lacks, well, an engineer's perspective."

He gave me his yes-I-completely-understand nod. "We must absolutely have a well-engineered escape plan. After dealing with

Mawbry in Britain, I'm starting to think that all these billionaires are dodgy types."

"Boy," I related, "me too. Dodgy and unstable. That's why our plan is to do this all carpe diem."

"Ah," Russell said, trying hard not to show his disapproval. "I see."

"Yeah," I said, "seize the moment when my first opportunity pops up to grab that little, solid-gold detonator away from Spiros. You know, snatch it out of his grasp when he least expects it."

"Yes, Sparks," Russell said, "I heard you—and you said it with such great portent, I might add. Now, may I inquire which of us will disarm the two goons with their nasty-looking assault weapons?"

"Funny," I said, totally hiding that I hadn't thought about that task, "I just considered asking you to take the goon standing on the left, and Britton, the one on the right."

Russell smiled. "Yes," he said, with the obvious knowledge that I'd just lied to him to save face. "I'm glad that I could nail that task down—*officially*, that is."

"Okay," I admitted, "it's true. I just assumed that when it came time to disarm the goons, Murphy, Lawrence, and James would be the actual action figures."

"Yes," Russell said, nodding. "Of course you did."

"Yeah," I agreed. "Just being me, I guess."

"And here I thought that you were irony impaired," Russell said, smiling. "Ironically, you, my dear mate, are always being you—assumptions and all."

"Ha-ha," I said, smirking. "By the way, old man," I added,

with a smug grin, "I assume you won't mind telling Britton that he's going to disarm the goon on his right?"

"No, Mr. Grumpy Pants." Russell smiled smugly. "I wouldn't mind at all. And to clarify, of course, I will be disarming the goon on my left."

"Fine with me," I said, shrugging. "However, it's possible that Murphy or the other two CIA agents might dismiss this part of the plan."

"No problem," he said. "I will simply discuss this with Murphy."

"Yeah," I said, "you do that." I took in a deep, steadying breath, then added, "Seriously, Russell, thanks for handling this integral part of the plan—obviously, disarming the two goons is crucial."

"You're welcome, Ethan," he said, attempting his friendly tone. "After all, we are a team, are we not?"

"Yes," I answered. "We are definitely a team. And an extremely elite one."

Chapter 37

"It's a very good plan," Hakim approved, with his Egyptian sensibility as usual, balancing it perfectly with his politeness.

"Thanks," I said, nodding. "I'm wondering, do you have a suggestion for how to further ensure the plan's success?"

"I do," Hakim said, in his very serious tone. "I suggest that in addition to your superb plan—that we add a password."

"You mean a signal word?" I said, nodding. "Just before I strike, I should yell out a let's-do-this-now signal word?"

"Precisely," Hakim said, with a respectful bow of his head.

"That's the signal word!" I told him. "Just before I strike, I'll yell out the word *precisely*."

Hakim smiled. You could tell that he liked my go-with-it style.

I looked at him. "Hakim," I asked, "will you take on the responsibility of informing the others of the signal word?"

"Yes," Hakim answered. "I would be honored to do so. You may depend on me, my friend."

"Oh yeah," I agreed. "I know this well. Tell me," I said, "what have you been up to lately?"

"Well," he began humbly, "I have been granted a scholarship to study Egyptology at the university in Cairo."

"Hakim," I exclaimed, "that's wonderful!"

"Thank you, my friend," he said, with a humble bow of his head. "What also makes this more wonderful is that my younger brother, Denesh, has agreed to take over the family shop for his career."

"Wow," I said, "perfect. Does Denesh know as much about spy equipment as you do?" I asked, remembering the cool spy shop that Hakim's family owned at the biggest mall in Cairo.

"Almost," Hakim answered, "but I teach him, and he learn very quickly."

"I'm so happy for you, Hakim. You'll be a famous Egyptologist someday."

"Thank you for saying so, Ethan," Hakim said, with that humble bow of his head.

"Hey," I uttered excitedly, suddenly thinking about it, "my dad loves Egyptology, as you know, and I'm sure that he would be honored to help you with your career goal anyway he can."

"Dr. Sparks has done so already," Hakim surprised me by saying. "Your father wrote a glowing reference for me to the university. I believe this most assuredly helped me to get my scholarship."

"Wow," I found myself saying, "I didn't know this."

"Perhaps you did not read my recent e-mail about this?"

"Um," I admitted, "no. I guess I got in the habit of texting Big Time lately, and now I sometimes forget to read my e-mails."

"Ah," Hakim uttered, "that explains it!"

Chapter 38

"Good idea, Double-O-Seven," Nico said, once I'd told him the updated plan. "A very good escape plan."

"Thanks, Double-O-Eight," I said, remembering our Greek adventure in Santorini with Evangalia and her little, yellow rowboat.

"How can I help?" Nico asked.

"Well," I said, "the moment you hear me call out the signal word *precisely*, you grab Pou-Pou. Just snatch him off Spiros's shoulder and contain the little turd."

"Very funny humor," Nico said, nodding. "Me grab the Pou-Pou."

"Yeah," I told him. "Grabbing the Pou-Pou is funny." I grinned. "Both funny and serious."

You do not have to remind me, my friend, Double-O-Seven, of how serious our desire is to take Spiros down again."

"Good," I said, "because this time when we take him down, we have to keep him down."

"Ah, yes, yes!" Nico exclaimed. "I did not know that Spiros got sprung from the jail! I am sure he bribed his way out."

"Do you still talk to his brother, Mandras?"

"Yes! Yes! Whenever I walk past his cave," Nico said. "He always invites me in to have a grape Fanta and an orange. We have very nice conversation."

"Do you talk about his brother, Spiros?" I inquired.

"No," he answered, "remember, I say we have very *nice* conversation. Talking about that no-good Spiros is very, very unpleasant, so we avoid doing so."

I nodded.

"Ethan, my very good friend," he said, "may I please ask you a personal question?"

"Of course," I said, shrugging. "Is your question about Evangalia?"

He nodded.

"You want to know if I want to be her boyfriend again?"

Another affirmative nod.

I sighed. "Before I answer your question, although I have the feeling that you already know the answer," I began, "may I first ask you a question?"

"Is your question to find out if I like Evangalia as a girlfriend for myself?"

"Yes."

Nico broke out in one of his great big smiles. "Do not worry, my friend," he assured me. "I like Evangalia very, very much, but only as a big brother likes his little sister."

"Oh," I said, suddenly feeling relieved, "then why do you want to know?"

"Because I am nosy," he informed me with a shrug and a grin.

As usual, Nico knew how to break the tension and make me laugh.

Chapter 39

After the last surveillance shift, I had a few minutes alone in the broom closet. Just enough time for my breathing to become erratic, so I concentrated on breathing in and out to steady my adrenalin and lower my pulse. I tried to focus on the steady ticking of my new military-grade watch to get my breathing under control, but with each minute that passed, I felt myself slipping into a pool of anxiety that would have easily drowned me if I let it drag me under.

I was definitely worried about everyone surviving the ordeal. The situation had way too many potential variables that could go wrong—any number of unexpected things that could turn on us, maybe even kill us.

I suddenly remembered that I had on the new pair of cargo pants my mom had bought me for this rescue mission. This pair of pants had an extra pocket, more like a hidden slit in the waistband, and stashed in this secret place I found our most recent family photo. *Family*, I realized, slowly managing to finally steady my breath. *I've spent the last two years annoyed by them, and if everything goes right, I'll be annoyed with them for decades to come.*

I snuck out of the broom closet and walked around the corner into the kitchen. I saw that only Spiros and my dad sat there, both drinking tea and talking, chatting really. Dad with a bomb strapped to his favorite yellow shirt with the two front pockets on each side, and Spiros with his nasty little monkey on his shoulder.

The only thing I can figure, I thought, *is their one commonality. The one thing they both respect and even adore: archaeological artifacts. Only my dad excavates them and Spiros, of course, steals them.*

"Ethan," Dad said, way too casually in my opinion. "Come join us. We're discussing the notorious history behind the Elgin Marbles."

"Okay," I said, grabbing a glass of OJ from a pitcher on the counter before sitting down. "Did anyone mention that the British Museum—no, actually the British government will not trade Dr. Sparks and his team for their Elgin Marbles?"

"Of course," Spiros said, "I know this. But I don't want the marbles anyway." He stopped. "Well, actually, I'm lying, I do want them, but even I know that I will never get them."

"Then this kidnapping really is all just about revenge. You're mad that we shut down your little artifact theft operation in Greece?"

"It's not entirely about my seeking revenge," Spiros said. "Oh yes, am I seething mad that you robbed me of my original collection back in Santorini?—absolutely! But the real reason I wanted you to come here is to see my new, even far more impressive collection! In fact, I am so proud of it that I am positively bursting to show it to you!"

"I don't care how impressive these artifacts are," I told him. "The fact is you stole them. They belong in a museum for everyone to see, not just for you and your hoity-toity friends to *oooh* and *ahhh* over!"

I looked over at my dad. The look of disapproval on his face warned me that poking the bear, a demented teddy bear in this case, might not be a good idea.

I turned to Spiros. "Okay, it's cards on the table time. Once we've seen your awesome collection, are you going to let us go?"

"For now, just know that I am very excited for you all to see my very rare, ancient archaeological artifacts," he said, obviously skirting my question. "I think you will appreciate them as much as I do." He paused, his thumb and index finger denoting a small amount. "Perhaps even a teeny-weenie bit more."

"I'm sure we will," I said, "but what then? Once you've shoved your impressive collection in our faces and said, 'nanna-nanna boo-boo,' are you going to let us go? You know, build another lair to hold up in and hide your impressive collection?"

"No," he said, feeding Pou-Pou a piece of melon from the little child's plate in front of him. "If I let you go, then you will no doubt spend your time obsessively tracking me down so the authorities can confiscate my beloved collection again."

"So," I asked, shrugging my shoulders, "then you are going to kill us all?"

"What choice do I have?" Spiros said, resigned to the fact

himself. "However," he added, looking at me disdainfully, "I must admit that it never occurred to me, Ethan, that you would show up with your entire entourage like this." His eyes threw daggers at me. "You have made my plan much more complicated," he said, muttering to himself. He looked up and glared at me. "Ethan, you are just naturally disruptive."

"Sorry for the inconvenience," I said, sarcastically.

"Oh, don't apologize, dear boy," the crazier part of Spiros said. "I will just make room aboard my supertanker *Sophia* for twelve more before I blow you all up at sea."

"So you were just kidding when you said that your chef, Theo, would be feeding us to the local hammerheads circling the island?"

"No," Spiros said, with a smug, upward twist of his chin. "Actually, I just changed my mind." He looked at me, his thin, manicured, sword-shaped eyebrows crossing as if they had become a plaque on the wall. "Blowing you all up here would be so messy. Poor Pou-Pou is getting so much older and might slip on all the blood. And of course, there is the preservation of my collection to consider." He paused, nodding decisively. "No, I will definitely blow you all up at sea—much, much cleaner." He slapped his little hands together with a loud clap. "No muss! No fuss!"

"Wow," I said, "talking to you is like playing bagpipes in a string quartet."

The "guests" started walking into the kitchen for breakfast, abruptly ending our conversation.

Chapter 40

The Antiquities Room had a 360-degree viewing area, oh the size of, let's say, a two-car garage. The private museum, as promised, turned out to be awesome—a climate-controlled, oval-shaped viewing space big enough to display thirty or so stolen artifacts. The archaeological artifacts all had custom-made pedestals or platforms. The room's air-conditioning was one of those dust-free systems that kept a constant sixty-degree temperature and prevented the carbon dioxide from our breath from touching the artifacts.

I counted twenty-eight archaeological artifacts; eighteen from Greece, five from Egypt, four from Neolithic China, including a Terra Cotta officer, and one from ancient Persia, an enormous horse that conjured up thoughts of the Trojan Horse. All these artifacts were priceless.

Very clever, I thought, watching everyone check out the artifacts. *Spiros plans to get us aboard a supertanker loaded with* natural gas. Then he will detonate the bombs, and the gas will accelerate the explosion.

The east Pacific is very remote. We won't be found right away, or at least the parts of us left after the massive explosion.

"Ethan," Lawrence said, "your father told Murphy about our pending transfer to the supertanker. James is in the process of informing the others of this. I got your message about the signal word, also that Russell and Britton will be taking out the goons. I think the signal word is a great idea. However, James and I will take out the goons, not Russell and Britton; it's too dangerous for civilians to do that."

"Okay," I said, nodding. "But Nico is still going to contain Pou-Pou, right?"

"Affirmative," Lawrence said. "As far as I know, Nico's instructions have not been changed. However, I did take the liberty of informing Russell and Britton of the change of plan that involves them."

"Ethan," Murphy said behind me, "I've received updates regarding our plan. I think we should quickly review them."

I nodded.

"We have the signal word, *precisely*," he began. "Lawrence and James are taking out the goons. And Nico is containing the vicious little monkey."

"Precisely," I said, in a vain attempt to lighten the mood—or at least mine.

"Well, I have something else I'd like to add to the plan," Murphy said, ignoring my attempt at humor.

"Shoot," I said.

"After Spiros and the two goons are contained," Murphy said, "I'm going to remove the bomb from your father and strap it on to Spiros."

"Ah, poetic justice," I said. "Let Spiros see what it feels like to have a bomb strapped to his chest. And to make it more poetic, I think Dad should get to hold the detonator."

"Good idea," Murphy proclaimed. "I agree, very poetic."

Chapter 41

As soon as we finished viewing the artifacts, the goons used their machine guns to immediately split us into two groups. Then each goon herded us onto two helicopters, poking us on our backs with their big assault weapons to make sure we understood that they were in control. In a precise, military-like maneuver, we were then whisked out to sea and deposited on board an enormous tanker ship.

One of the transport helicopters flew away, leaving the other one standing idly on the fan deck's helipad. My guess, that helicopter could only hold eighteen comfortably. We were twenty-two. *A tight fit but doable*, I thought, continuously assessing our carpe diem plan.

There were twenty-two of us versus six of them: Spiros, his two goons, a server, the ship's captain, and his one crewmember. I wasn't counting the miserable little monkey that seemed super-glued to Spiros's shoulder.

We were being "escorted" to *Sophia's* luxurious, oversized back fan deck. A truly tricked-out deck that had an enormous round table, complete with a linen tablecloth, matching napkins, fancy-looking plates, and gold utensils. Twinkling, little white lights strung on walls made of garden trellis, and the billowy overhead canopy that looked like a ginormous silk handkerchief worked hard at creating a festive ambience. Instead of candles on the table, we each had our own little nightclub-looking lamp with a tiny, pinkish-red glow emanating from it.

Circling the table, I dropped Dad's seasick pills off at his place. The bottle he'd used as a visual clue back on Easter Island.

Dad looked up and nodded his thanks to me. I saw a glint of pride in his eyes.

Boy, I thought, deliberately sitting next to our five-foot host with a prosthetic right leg and a spider monkey on his shoulder at the head of his elegant dinner table, *Spiros can really be a diva sometimes.*

Once we were seated, the servers started pouring a fruity-looking drink for the minors and wine for the adults.

We are not going to die tonight, I thought. *This is not going to be our last supper.*

"My," I suddenly heard Spiros's squeaky, annoying voice say in my ear, "aren't we deep in thought?"

I turned to him and said, "What can I say? One can get pensive when one's loved ones are in danger."

"Or perhaps," Spiros said, "you're figuring out your plan of escape. I know that is what I would be doing if I had a family that I loved and wanted to protect."

"But you don't," I reminded him. "Even your little brother, Mandras, can't stand you."

Spiros laughed. "And you think this bothers me?"

"No," I said, shrugging my shoulders. "I know that you love things much more than you love people."

Abruptly, the first course arrived before us. An enormous shrimp cocktail served in a heavy-looking crystal bowl chock full of shaved ice.

I looked over at Dad, talking to Rolf, his official photographer and my thirty-two-year-old friend, whose wife, Dr. Sarum, was pregnant with twins. And Murphy, good old, dependable, loyal Murphy—he sat right there, right next to my dad.

Boy I am so glad that I love people more than things, I thought to myself.

"Well," Spiros asked, condescendingly, "do you think we'll actually get to the second course before you and your entourage begin your rescue plan?"

"No," I answered. "In fact, we will not even complete this course."

I quickly glanced over at Drew and gave him our secret sign. He threw one of the enormous shrimps at Pou-Pou. It hit the little monkey right between his eyes, and he started shrieking wildly.

This of course distracted Spiros, so I yelled out our signal word, *precisely*! Then I picked up my extremely heavy, lead-and-crystal shrimp-cocktail bowl and hit Spiros smack on his chest with it. He doubled over in abject pain, and as he did, I carefully removed the solid-gold detonator that he had strapped to his wrist just like a girl has a corsage strapped to her wrist for prom.

I held up the detonator, deliberately keeping it as far away from Spiros as possible. Then I just sat back in my seat and relaxed by breathing steadily in and out until my heart stopped drilling through my chest.

In a semi-fog of surreal haziness, I viewed a glorious outburst of chaos. As I started to come down from my adrenalin high, I had to force myself to remain focused on only watching the unfolding of our collaborative escape plan.

My job, now done, had been to initiate the carpe diem start of the plan. Then, one by one, the other team members involved took their cues from each other and executed their assigned steps in the process. It took an enormous effort of self-discipline on my part not to jump in and take over the other team members' jobs. I even had to fight a flash of rationalization within myself that asked, *Where would we be if all we did was what we were supposed to do?*

In order to do this, I actually had to deliberately pretend that a slow-motion video streamed before my eyes. I watched Lawrence and James disarm the two goons, now pointing the assault weapons at them, instead of the other way around. Then Nico, both of his hands protectively wrapped in a pair of socks that he'd hidden in his pocket for this occasion, snatched Pou-Pou from Spiros's shoulder so he could strap the creepy little monkey into a kid's highchair that Spiros always kept on hand when it proved necessary to put his "child" in time-out. At this point, I warned Spiros that if he tried anything that I would personally take his baby's highchair, monkey and all, and fling it into the ocean. To be honest, I wasn't sure if my threat was a bluff or not, but I definitely made it sound like it wasn't.

Once Spiros, his monkey, and the two goons were contained, Murphy triumphantly, *poetically* even, marched over to transfer the bomb from my dad to Spiros as planned.

When Murphy bent over to start unhooking Dad's bomb jacket, we heard Spiros suddenly say, "Ah, Murphy, I wouldn't do that if I were you."

"Why not?" Murphy demanded.

"Because, in preparation of your expected shenanigans," Spiros answered, "I deliberately had my tech experts rig the good doctor's digital bomb—so should anyone try to remove it—it will automatically detonate."

Chapter 42

"Ah, Spiros," I asked, "did you rig everyone's bomb to automatically go off this way?"

"No," Spiros answered, "just your father's, Ethan."

With that, the three CIA agents started to remove the bombs from the others one by one, throwing each and every one of them as far out into the ocean as they could.

Suddenly Spiros started laughing, a very unnerving laugh. The kind of laugh when you truly think you have the upper hand.

"What?" I insisted, glaring at one of the most annoying people that I know.

Spiros stopped laughing. Then he reared his eyes up at me and said, "Well, I've only told you half of my plan B."

"I know you're anxious to tell me the other half," I told him.

"Well, yes I am," he readily admitted.

I waited.

"Well?" I insisted, barely holding onto my cool.

"Not until you give me my Pou-Pou back," Spiros said with a theatrical fake smile.

I looked over at Nico and nodded. Double-O-Eight wheeled Spiros's precious little Pou-Pou over to him.

The creepy spider monkey jumped up and down in his highchair, but the chair's specially outfitted harness kept the little cretin contained as it had been designed to do.

"Part two of plan B," I reminded him.

"Yes," Spiros said, still with his smug smile, only it had started becoming more twisted, more menacing, like he'd been savoring the moment for as long as he could. I started to silently count the seconds ... and got up to thirteen.

"Now!" I shouted. "Either you tell me what your lame plan B is right now—or your darling little Pou-Pou is going for a swim!"

"Okay! Okay!" Spiros yelled, throwing both of his hands up in the air as if I was the one being unreasonable. "I think you should know that I also had my techs install a timer in Dr. Sparks's bomb."

"Have you already activated the timing mechanism in Dr. Sparks's bomb?" Murphy demanded, staring directly at Spiros.

"I do not know," Spiros answered, both hands up, shrugging his shoulders as if he really wasn't sure.

"All right," Murphy said, barely able to hold onto his anger. "Let's do it this way," he continued, managing to level out a bit, "either you tell me everything you know about the activation of Dr. Sparks's fun-size bomb—or I'll throw your deranged monkey into the Pacific Ocean myself. And I'll even throw all these extremely heavy crystal shrimp bowls into a sack and tie it around Pou-Pou's neck so he'll sink so fast you won't even have the time to say bye-bye."

Spiros's smugness visibly crumbled into fear. He looked up at Murphy. "All right! All right! I will tell you what I know!"

"Now," Murphy insisted, walking over, picking up the highchair with its strapped-in monkey, and carrying it over to the deck rail. "You have thirty seconds to tell Agents Lawrence and James," he continued. "They're both bomb experts."

"That's right, Murphy," Spiros said, his smugness starting to creep back in. "In your day, you weren't much of a bomb expert back then, were you?"

"Not the clever miniaturization that the techs have managed to come up with today," Murphy admitted, shrugging.

"Fair enough," Spiros actually said. "Yes." He nodded affirmatively. "It is definitely high-tech these days." He looked up. "I am afraid that I am not so high-tech myself," he said, with his theatrical fake smile.

"Okay," Murphy said, just barely holding on, "enough of the bonding. Tell Lawrence and James the details about the activation of Dr. Sparks's bomb." The big, bull-necked man held the monkey in his highchair up over the rail. All he had to do was let go—and the monkey would become shark food.

"All right! All right!" Spiros yelled out, and started to beg. "Please, please do not hurt him." He caught his breath. "What I know is simple really." He looked over at Lawrence and James. "I may have inadvertently activated the good doctor's bomb—when Ethan surprised me by snatching the detonator from me. I'm not sure, but I think I might have pushed the activation button on my new high-tech wristwatch by accident."

"Okay," Murphy said, dangling the monkey up and down over the rail. "Did you or did you not 'accidentally' push the activation button?"

"Um, I think I did," Spiros finally answered.

"How much time remains till it blows up?"

"Oh, I believe about thirty-five minutes or so. I'm not 100 percent sure," Spiros answered. "I, um, actually did not think this plan B of mine through well enough."

"Well," I said, "you thought that after activating Dr. Sparks's bomb, you'd be taking off in your helicopter and only leaving *us* to die."

"Yes," Spiros admitted. "This is true."

"Well," I said, "things have changed, haven't they? It seems that you have a decision to make now. Either you help us disarm my father's bomb—or you'll die right along with us."

"Well," Spiros said, sounding dead serious, "since I know nothing about the schematics of the bomb, except that it has a timer rigged to start accelerating if someone tries to disarm it, it seems *all* of our lives are in Agent Lawrence's and Agent James's hopefully capable hands."

Chapter 43

"Do not panic," Lawrence informed us after examining the bomb. "James and I have disarmed this type of digital bomb in less than eighteen minutes."

"Yes," James confirmed. "Seventeen and a half minutes is our record to date."

"Good," I said, "but by my current calculation, that's two minutes less than we have in our present situation."

"Affirmative," James said, nodding the appropriate gesture of understanding in these types of situations. "So, therefore, in this actual field maneuver, we will simply have to upgrade our previous performance level."

"Yes," I agreed, sighing. "You will definitely have to beat your old record or we will all die."

"Affirmative," Lawrence answered, already at work. "The first thing to do is to ascertain the correct wire to cut so I can remove the bomb without it blowing up." The special agent in charge then paused—a long, unnerving pause that clearly gave you the impression that there was a *but* coming. "But," he finally added, "there is the chance that the mechanism that'll make the bomb blow if you remove it from Dr. Sparks is also the same mechanism that will cause the timer to immediately start accelerating as well."

"We'll just have to take that chance," Murphy said, sighing. "At least once the bomb has been safely removed from Dr. Sparks, we can pitch it out into the Pacific." He paused, another *but* pause. "Hopefully the bomb won't explode before I can throw it overboard."

I glanced over at our bomb squad. "Ah," I asked, "if both the removal and timer mechanisms are connected, is it possible to remove my father's bomb in time to throw it out far enough into the ocean?"

"Well," Lawrence said, closely examining the motion trigger on the bomb strap, "I have to tell you, I see two default triggers."

"Three," James said, looking up from his examination. "There are three default triggers. One is hidden. I believe it may be a decoy."

"Decoy?" Russell, the genius engineer asked. "As in a hidden trigger that will override the other two?"

James turned to him. "Yes," he confirmed, "I believe so."

"You're not absolutely sure?" Lawrence asked.

"No," James answered, "I'm afraid that I am not 100 percent sure."

"Ah," I said, "percentage wise, how sure are you?"

James looked up. "Well, let's say 90 percent sure."

Lawrence turned to us. "Perhaps we should downgrade that to

fifty-fifty," he said. "There's the possibility that once we cut any of the possible three hot wires, it will cause a rapid acceleration in the timed triggering of the bomb. That's the latest MO we're seeing with these types of new personal-sized digital bombs."

I turned to Spiros.

"Don't look at me, Ethan," he protested. "I do not know. I told you, I am not tech-savvy. This is why I employ others who are."

"I suggest that given our limited time frame at present," Russell said, "it would behoove us to cut the decoy wire and simply hope for the best."

"Affirmative," Lawrence agreed, nodding, "especially with the possible acceleration factor. We may literally only have two seconds to remove the bomb from Dr. Sparks's chest and dispose of the device safely overboard."

With that, the agent in charge took a Swiss Army knife out of his pocket, opened up the scissors section, and cut the decoy wire. Suddenly, a timer loudly clicked on, and the frantic sound of acceleration cut through the air, getting the last laugh!

Chapter 44

Lawrence's hands were a blur as he unbuckled all three straps and finally removed the bomb from around my father's chest.

Murphy dove in, grabbed the bomb from Lawrence's hands, then ran across the enormous back deck and threw the explosive device high over the *Sophia's* closest railing just as it exploded Big Time!

The bomb's explosion shook the ship so violently that several of us were thrown across the deck, me included. Ironically, I grabbed onto Pou-Pou's highchair; the chair banged into the deck railing and actually stopped me from sliding underneath the bottom rail and flying into the ocean.

Suddenly a fiery piece of the detonated bomb shot up from the surface of the ocean. This miniature firebomb flew into the billowy silk canopy over our heads. Immediately a fire broke out on board, started spreading, and threatened to travel over and blow up the gassed-up helicopter.

Everyone ran toward the common goal of putting out the fire overhead. The blaze had quickly caught on and intensified. Soon the entire billowy silk dining canopy became ablaze, perhaps giving us only a few minutes until the demented fire started lapping at the helipad, causing our rescue copter to blow sky high.

Adrenalin must have kicked in because when I returned from grabbing the closest deck hose, everyone seemed to be doing a great job working toward diverting the fire away from the helipad deck.

The length of the hose fell short by about twenty feet from my intended target area. Abruptly, the length of the hose just stopped, and I snapped back like a rubber band, bounced a few times, and finally fell down hard on my tailbone.

I ignored the multiple stabs of pain in my backside, jumped up and let go of the pinched-closed elbow that I had made in the hose so I could run with it. Then I aimed the now-open blast of water into the closest part of the fire that the hose and I could reach.

It took a while, but finally I managed to start containing an end piece of the spread-out blaze.

Soon, everyone concentrated solely on their individual piece of the fire, all of us working separately but as a cohesive team with one objective.

While I worked the hose blast, the rest of our fire team used buckets that they had to keep filling at a nearby faucet.

It took a while until our hard work finally managed to start controlling the overhead blaze.

Finally, our efforts extinguished the fire. I turned to Spiros and asked, "Is there anything we need to know about the rescue helicopter?" I took in a breath to calm myself. Then clarified, "Except for the obvious fact that it's a transport helicopter that seats eighteen, and we are twenty-two."

"Twenty-four actually," Spiros corrected me. "You forgot Pou-Pou and me."

"What about your five employees on board with you at this time?"

Spiros leaned in and whispered, "They are expendable."

"Wow," I said, not caring that I was being obviously judgmental, "I am appalled that you think your employees are expendable. Appalled but not surprised." I shook my head back and forth.

I looked the five-foot billionaire with his prosthetic leg right in the eye. "I'm not surprised," I said. "Where you have employees, we have friends."

Spiros stared at me and shot, "Well then, dear Ethan, I hope you count me and Pou-Pou as two of your friends, because the helicopter in question requires a ten-digit code to turn it on." He smugly paused. "You know, to activate the ignition button."

"Of course it does," I said, "and you won't tell us what that code is unless we take you with us."

"Yes, Ethan, very good deduction. You are a truly gifted detective," Spiros Stepanopolis said, sounding sincere. "In a way, you remind me of Sherlock Holmes. I've read all the Holmes books, you know."

"Well," Drew said, shrugging his shoulders, "that's nice, Spiros, but I know the ten-digit code. You wrote it down on a piece of paper that I found in your kitchen so you wouldn't forget it."

"So," Spiros said, smirking, "and you think you remember all ten digits?"

"Yes," Drew told him. "I have a photographic memory. All I have to do is see something once, and I remember it."

The smirk on Spiros's face collapsed. "Still," he whined, "you're going to let me come with you, aren't you?"

Not answering him almost made him cry. "Please, Ethan," my pocket nemesis begged. "How do I know that I can trust you?"

"Oh, I'm sorry," I said, holding my little finger down to him. "Would you like me to pinky swear?"

Spiros surprised me by answering, "Yes, that would work."

"Speaking of things that work," I told him, "this time you'll be in a prison in the US. Kidnapping American citizens is a federal crime there. A life sentence," I added, smiling, "especially when you endanger law enforcement officers working for the FBI in the process."

Chapter 45

Carefully, all twenty-eight people and one little monkey began boarding the rescue helicopter built for eighteen passengers.

This exacting procedure started seeming hopeless around passenger twenty-two. A coincidence? No, I don't believe in coincidences. So no, it wasn't a coincidence. Nor would we take off without the six bad guys and the hateful monkey.

It would be a violation of our code. The good-guy honor code. The captain of the *Sophia* informed us that we might have managed to put out the deck blaze, but the fire had travelled below deck and had started heading for the gas tanks. The captain estimated the ship would be exploding in less than fifteen minutes, and the coast guard, already on its way, estimated their arrival as being in twenty-six minutes. So, no fatal bloodshed—neither good guy nor bad.

I watched Lawrence and James stack passengers twenty-three, -four, -five, and -six in the cargo hold in the rear of the helicopter as if they were luggage.

Then the agent in charge barely closed and locked us sardines into its tin can. Then he and James took posts outside the helicopter, one on each of the expansive side rails that flanked both sides of the overfilled craft actually managing to get all twenty-eight souls on board.

I looked out the steamed-up window, first to my left, then my right. It appeared that Agents Lawrence and James had secure footholds on the helicopter's railings, and their hands seemed secure in the door jams on each side of the craft.

Murphy, sitting in the pilot's seat, turned to Drew. "The ten-digit ignition code, please."

"Eight-six-two-six-three-six-two-six-four-six," Drew rattled off. Spiros glared at him.

Murphy typed in the ten-digit code, then pushed in the ignition button. The helicopter roared to life. Since we were a combined payload of about 5,800 or so pounds in a maximum capacity of 6,000 pounds allowed, the dual-bladed helicopter sputtered and struggled with its initial ascent. For a moment, it felt like we weren't gonna make it up.

Essentially, it took a wing and a prayer to get the overstuffed helicopter up to a cruising altitude.

When it had, I turned to Murphy and asked, "How many miles to the nearest coast guard substation?"

"It's 6.9 miles due true north," Murphy answered.

Obviously relieved by this information, the passengers broke out in a chorus of nervous chatter—with a newfound optimism and in celebration of a successful end to our extremely important mission.

I looked next to me on my right. Evangalia sat beside me. Face to face like this, I noticed that she had an all-knowing smile on her beautiful lips.

So to surprise the always all-knowing, cute, and totally babe-like Evangalia—I swooped in and kissed those beautiful lips.

"Gotcha!" I exclaimed.

"Yes," she said. "But you are on probation."

I turned to face her. "Shhhh …" I said, index finger to my mouth. "Hear that wind—it says throw caution to me."

Then *boom!* went the supertanker below us.

Um, I realized, *we just had a kumbaya moment.*

Epilogue

The first spypartner on my scheduled list to personally thank turned out to be Anya.

"I hope we can still be friends," Anya said, totally surprising me. Then I immediately felt the relief of not having to initiate a breakup with her.

"Well," she insisted, "you have nothing to say?"

"How did you know?" I asked, my feeling of relief collapsing into the realization that this had become an awkward situation after all.

Anya looked at me. "Of course you are kidding?"

I stared at her, not knowing what to say.

"Do you not think that everyone knows that you and Evangalia have fallen back in love again?"

"Jack told you," I said, not so surprised anymore.

"Of course Jack told me," Anya said, hand on hip, that wonderful sarcastic smile of hers on her beautiful Mexican face. "Is he not one of the *everyone* that I just spoke of? So, I will ask you again, are you kidding?"

Oh-oh, I thought. *Here comes the heat.*

I took in a deep breath and then let it out slowly ... "Are you mad at me?"

"Do I look mad?" she said, answering my question with another question.

"Yes," I answered.

"All right," she said, with a grin. "At first I may have been a little mad at you." She paused, biting her lower lip, then looked up. "But I am l not so mad anymore."

"Good," I said, back to feeling relief, "then we can part friends?"

"Yes …"

"I'm glad about that," I confided, "because it would upset me Big Time if we couldn't."

"Me too," she said, admitting it with one of her sentimental smiles. All of her expressive smiles, frowns, and grins had become so familiar to me—even, well, endearing.

Then Anya looked up. Her smile turned from sentimentality to mischievousness right before my eyes. "Besides, if falling back in love with your last girlfriend becomes a toxic pattern for you, then you are in luck, because as your friend, I'll be able to point it out to you, perhaps even help you through such a disaster in the making by turning you down."

"I see your point," I told her, grinning.

"Good," she said, her smile going on and off like it had a loose connection. "Now I can forgive you, and we can move on and become friends."

"Yes," I said, nodding gratefully. "I'm so glad that we can become friends."

"Me too," she said, leaning over and kissing me on the cheek.

Then Anya turned and walked off, backpack in hand, to her departure gate.

She didn't look back.

Not even as a friend.

I suppose that will take time.

"Listen, dude, like I always say," Jack said, barely seconds into my second scheduled so-long, "it's much healthier to acknowledge your feelings than deny them."

"I don't know if that font of wisdom is more *chick* or *Californian*," I told him. "More *New Age* or *modern*."

"Proof," he said, "that labels don't work."

"Speaking of labels," I admitted, "do you have a new one? You know, something to update on your Facebook page?"

"No," he readily admitted. "She shot me down. Bang-bang," he added, dramatically clutching his heart. Despite the bravado, I knew he felt disappointed.

"And how do you feel?" I asked, trying very hard not to be a smart ass. "You know, 'it's healthier to acknowledge your feelings, than deny them,' as you say."

"All right," he confided, "Anya may have shot me down, arrow right through the heart and all, but at least we're still good friends." He paused and looked down at his sandals. "Maybe now you and I can finally be better friends because we're not competing for the same babe."

"Yeah," I said, offering him a fist-bump. "I'd like that."

The fist-bump he returned honestly seemed sincere. Apparently both of us not dating Anya at least turned out to be really beneficial to our friendship. And it seemed Jack was redeemable, like a coupon.

Wow, I realized, *two guys both liking the same girl makes it impossible for both dudes to be good friends. I guess Drew and I are lucky that we both never liked the same girl.*

Next came Chen-Jun.

"Wow," I told him, "I have to tell you I really like working with you."

"Thank you," he said, with a sincere bow of his head. "It is always an honor to work with you as well, my very good friend."

"As you know," I began, "this mission turned out to be all-consuming. So I'm glad that I finally have this opportunity to talk about the fact that you're going to Beijing Normal University this coming fall."

"Well," Chen-Jun said, leaning in and with a lower voice, "to be honest with you, I am feeling both excited and dismayed. I'm excited because I scored so high on the exam and made my parents so very, very proud. And of course being able to go to college to study de-extinction is a dream come true. However, despite all this good news, I, well, I feel a little dismayed because I'm, I'm, well a little bit worried."

"Worried," I repeated. "What about?"

"It is silly really," he said, looking down at his shoes.

"Maybe not," I said. "But I won't know until you tell me a bit more about what has you feeling worried."

"Yes," Chen-Jun said, glancing up. "Of course, my good friend, E-than, you are correct. I should tell you."

I waited.

"So I will," he continued. "I am worried a bit about my youth, only being fourteen years old and already enrolled in college. I am not mature like the others who will be attending college this fall."

"Then I guess you *are* being silly," I told him, "because you are definitely mature already. I bet that you're probably more mature than most of the seventeen-year-olds that'll be starting at Beijing Normal University this coming fall."

"Yes, my good friend. You are most correct."

"It's only correct," I said, "if the central truth is accepted and that truth has the power to lessen the unfounded worry."

"Again, you are *most* correct, my friend."

"Yeah," I admitted, "that and the fact that it takes one to know one, as they say."

"You mean being an individual prone to worry?" Chen-Jun asked, seeking clarity, "or being very, very mature for your age?"

"Both," I answered.

"Yes," Chen-Jun said, "how true. How very, very true."

Number four on the So-long List turned out to be Russell.

"Well, Ethan," the seventeen-year-old genius started, "it's back to being a highly respected engineer again."

He gave me a fake stiff-upper-lip smile and then added, "You know, Sparks, as opposed to being a secret agent whenever I'm around you."

"You're welcome," I said, nodding. "I'm glad that you really like being a covert operator once in a while."

"Yes," he acknowledged, "of course our very own James Bond, 007, is obviously the root cause of my secret-agent obsession." He looked up. "You know, while I was stuck in that awkward phase of growing up."

"All right," I said, "I'll pretend that I don't know how much you like being a real secret agent whenever you're around me."

"See that you don't, Sparks," Russell said, seriously. "However, I expect a call from you every time the need for a spypartner presents itself again."

"I hope you have a lot of vacation time," I said, grinning.

"Yes," he said, smiling. "I do. I may have told you, I have my own engineering firm now—have so for four months now."

"I receive all your monthly bulletins," I reminded him. "I'm on your mailing list."

"I know," he said, his big ears wiggling in camaraderie. "I just wasn't sure if you read them or not. I thought that you had," he said, "but I wasn't really sure."

"Are you sure that you weren't sure?" I asked. "You are one of the most self-aware people I know."

"That's only because I have chosen to demonstrate this trait while on secret-agent missions with you."

"Yeah," I said, "well then that explains a lot."

"I'm pleased that I could provide further explanation of myself to you," he said, the ring of sincerity in his voice belying the words that exited his mouth. Then he added, "Ethan, I truly do appreciate the fact that whenever I'm around you, I get the opportunity to go on an exhilarating covert operation." He bent down and whispered, "I may not show it, but being an engineer is not always as exciting as it sounds. I truly do appreciate the, well, disruption in pattern, shall we say, that you provide for me."

"You're welcome," I said, grinning. "And I really appreciate the skills that you bring to the table."

"And I thank you," he said, "for inviting me to the table."

"Seems, even though there's a three-year age difference between us," I said, "we are definitely good friends."

"Yes," he said, "that is a puzzle, isn't it?"

"No," I said, suddenly serious, "the reason for this is not a puzzle to me. I believe it all boils down to mutual respect."

Russell laughed.

"I wasn't being funny," I said.

"Yes, I know," he told me. "That is why I am laughing."

"You think it's funny that I'm being serious?"

"No," he answered. "It's more a nervous laughter, possibly a rude trait of mine when one of my mates gets, well, sentimental."

"Wow," I pointed out, "you're weird."

"I imagine to a Yank," he countered, "that I would no doubt seem that way."

This time, I laughed. Whether he was being serious or not, I found it funny.

"Well, so long for now, my good friend," Hakim began with a slight bow of his head. Not Asian; more Egyptian in its style.

"Guess what?" I asked him. "My mother invited you to our Ocracoke summer house for the Fourth of July. And it's less than two months from today."

"I know!" Hakim said, excitedly. "My parents received and

approved your mother's gracious handwritten invitation three weeks ago."

"I know," I admitted. "I guess I'm just glad that since I have to say so long to everyone like this, with you, I get to say see ya real soon."

"Not to beat a dead camel," Hakim said, "but I know this as well. You are very sentimental, my friend."

"I knew that you also knew this," I said, just before I started laughing.

Hakim laughed right along with me.

It's so easy hanging out with Hakim, I realized. *No wonder I picked him when Drew cancelled Fourth of July in Ocracoke this year and Mom told me that I got to pick one of my other friends to replace him.*

The next two so-longs scheduled on the list surprised me by coming to say good-bye together. Nico and Evangalia.

"Hey, guys," I said, trying not to show how disappointed I felt that I wouldn't get to say so long to them individually. "I wasn't expecting you both at the same time."

"Yes," Evangalia freely admitted, "we know this."

"Huh," I said, stalling for time to try to figure out why Evangalia made Nico come along with her. "What's wrong, Evangalia? You don't want to be alone with me?"

"I do," she said. "However, since it seems that we are starting to court again, my culture insists that I should bring along an escort with me."

"I see," I said, trying hard not to show how amused this made me. "Then it's official, we're dating again."

"Yes, Double-O-Seven," Nico said, "it is official."

"Thank you, Nico, for making that clear," I said.

"You're welcome, my friend," he said, barely able not to bust out in laughter.

"Go ahead," Evangalia interjected, throwing her hands up. "You boys want to laugh, so laugh."

So we did, all three of us. It immediately brought back that wonderful summer adventure we had in Santorini, Greece.

Evangalia stopped laughing. She looked at me. "Oh, Ethan, I have missed you."

"I've missed you too," I told her. "Big time."

"Music to my ears," Evangalia said.

"Yes," Nico agreed, both hands up in the air, "a symphony, actually."

Then we broke out in another of our many mutual laugh fests.

Suddenly something occurred to me. "Hey!" I blurted out. "I still have some job savings left. I would love to spend it by coming for a three- or four-week visit to Santorini this summer."

"This would make me very, very happy," Evangalia said, sounding very, very happy.

"And me as well," Nico said. Then he paused, looked up at me with a mischievous smile, and added, "I am sure that my family would be happy to invite you to stay at *my* house."

"Yes," I said with a grin, "I'm sure they would."

Britton, my new Aussie friend, came last but not least on the list.

"Well, mate," the nineteen-year-old opened with, "I am already looking forward to our next adventure."

"So am I," I said, pointing up. "My anticipation is actually leaning toward a guided Himalayan adventure." I gave him the wait-for-it eye. "Ah, seems my dad has an archaeological dig scheduled in Kathmandu this fall. If you're free, I'd like to invite you to join me."

"Well, that'll work, mate," he said, grinning. "Thankfully, I'm no longer afraid of heights. So, the Himalayas, here we come!"

"I have always wanted to climb the Himalayas," I told him.

"So have I, mate," Britton said. "So have I."

"I hope you're serious," I said, "because I am." I looked at him. "Like you, I used to be afraid of heights too. But now I'm more afraid of the lows."

"That's what I like most about you, mate," Britton said. "You're relevant."

"Yeah," I said, nodding. "I get it. That's what I like most about you too."

"So looks like there's another adventure to come, huh?"

"Definitely! It's either that," I confided, "or I'll have to start *reliving* them, because I can't live without them."

"You're preachin' to the choir, mate," he told me. "I own an adventure company in Machu Picchu, remember?"

"It's hard to forget that," I said. "My guess, you're like me; it's in your DNA."

"Actually, mate, both of my parents are unassuming schoolteachers."

"My father is a geeky archaeologist, and my mother is a

cookbook author with her own foodie show on the Cooking Network," I pointed out. "Still, look at us. Our ancestors must have been adventurers. It's too much a part of who we are."

"Bottom line, I think," he said, shrugging, "is that we dream big and make it happen." He paused and looked up. "You know, mate," he said, as if just thinking about it, "I think you've just had an epiphany shine down upon you. Seems it's become apparent that you have just been shown that it's perfectly okay to love your family and yet completely still be your own person."

"Uh," I reflected. "An epiphany like that does take a lot of pressure off me."

"Um," he said, nodding. "It does, doesn't it?"

"Oh yeah," I answered, "it definitely does."

"I had a recent epiphany as well," Britton confided. "You can't choose your destiny. You can only fulfill it—or fail it."

"Wow," I said, nodding my head. "That is so true."

Um, I realized, *I think I just had a seminal moment.*

Made in the USA
Middletown, DE
12 September 2015